Sarah Al Shafei comes from an island in the Middle East known as the Kingdom of Bahrain. She studied in Boston and Miami and graduated with a BA in Liberal Arts. She is a constant traveller and enjoys writing short stories and poetry at the same time. She is a monthly correspondent in a local English woman's magazine where she writes about real life stories in the Arab world. *Yummah* is her first novel. She is a twenty-four-year-old housewife and currently lives with her husband, Mohammed, and her two daughters, Noor and Dana, in Jeddah, Saudi Arabia.

YUMMAH

YUMMAH

Sarah A. Al Shafei

ATHENA PRESS
LONDON

YUMMAH
Copyright © Sarah A. Al Shafei 2005

All Rights Reserved

No part of this book may be reproduced in any form
by photocopying or by any electronic or mechanical means,
including information storage and retrieval systems,
without permission in writing from both the copyright
owner and the publisher of this book.

ISBN 1 84401 368 5

First Published 2005 by
ATHENA PRESS
Queen's House, 2 Holly Road
Twickenham TW1 4EG
United Kingdom

Printed for Athena Press

To my Yummah
You are truly my muse

All characters and events in this book are fictional in their entirety. Any resemblance to actual people, living or dead, is purely coincidental.

Chapter One

I was twelve years old, still a kid with fairy-tale dreams and never-ending imaginings. My favorite toy was still a doll, Layla, in my arms day and night. And my mama's lap was still my true home. My father, Abdullah, had died a long time ago; Mama told me once that we never met for he died in a storm that hit the Indian Ocean as he was returning from India where he was in a business trip, right before I was born. I had two brothers, Aziz and Hassan, who both left the country in search for work, and I was the only girl, Mama's girl.

I lived in Bahrain, a beautiful tropical island in the Middle East, east of Saudi Arabia, south of Iran. It was a place like no other, known to be the mother of a million palm trees. It was a small island under the British rule but we kept our culture and tradition alive, our religion was our pride, and our life was simple and trouble free. We all knew each other, like one big family and we were happy. The sun was always shining, the sky was always clear. It rained in autumn and spring was my favorite time.

I had a good life. My father had been a clever businessman in his lifetime, always planning for the worst. He made sure his family had enough to survive if something would happen to him, "as if he knew what was to happen," my mother would say. Both my brothers didn't go to school but had teachers and tutors come to them at home. That was how the wealthy were educated back then. My mother, on the other hand, tutored me. I was taught how to sew, how to cook, how to take care of a household. I was taught how to present myself, how to talk, to laugh, to walk and all the things that would come in the etiquette package, I guess; therefore I never got to read or write, which was the only thing I regret. I had a good life.

My house, or actually my mother's house, was a big house. It had four bedrooms, two bathrooms, two kitchens, two living rooms and two dining rooms, for the men and women ate separately in the company of guests. We had a huge courtyard, which we called *housh*, that had our private water well. The courtyard also had a brick oven where the maids baked the Bahraini bread we called *khubis khabaz*.

★

It was a bright summer day; I was the only one out in the courtyard. The weather was too hot for anyone to stay outside but I was too tired of the nonstop women talk inside. Layla and I decided to have tea party and because Mama wouldn't allow me to play with real cups I had to use small rocks for cups and a big rock for the tea pot (there weren't any toy cups and pots back then). You might think that twelve years old is a bit too old for a tea party but in my days the twelve-year-olds were still innocent, their eyes still had their childish sparkle and their hearts were pure as angels'.

"Khadeeja, leave that doll and come in at once... You are not a child any more, you are getting married!" cried my mother.

Married. The word kept echoing in my head and my heart skipped a beat. Leave the doll. Layla? How can I leave Layla? She's been with me as far as I can remember. What is Mama talking about? There were so many questions in my head that I ignored my mother's call without noticing her standing in front of me. I was confused and something inside me was aching for someone to say that it was all a joke, aching for someone to give me back my Layla and tell me that we'll stay together forever but all I saw was my mama's angry face and women waiting for a reaction in the background.

Mama pulled me by the hand into an adjacent room where we could be alone for a moment. She walked across the room and as she sat down slowly I realized for the first time how old she looked, even though she was young in age. The difficult times since my father's death left its marks on her beautiful face and her hands seemed so thin and wrinkled. Her once-beautiful body now looked heavy and weak and her arm had a constant shake. I never knew what losing a loved one could do to a person until I saw Mama. My Aunt Jameela told me once how close my parents had been. Mama would wait every day by the door for Baba's return and when their eyes met Mama would have a magical shine on her face. Her pretty nonstop smile was nowhere to be seen now and I longed to hear her laugh as I was told she used to. Mama left everyone believing that when Baba died, he took all that was beautiful in her with him.

"Khadeeja you are twelve years old now, you are not a child any more. I am sick, Khadeeja, and I don't know how long I have left, I want to see you in safe hands, baby. Your two brothers are happily married but if something happened to me, I don't want to leave you a burden on your brothers. Khadeeja, I know you are used to my protection but you have to learn how to rely on yourself. Make sure that I won't give you to just anyone, for you are more precious to me than anything in this world. The man I chose to wed you is a good man. He is old enough to take care of you, he is educated and well off. You were wanted by many, Khadeeja, but I chose the best and you are to get married this Thursday."

"Mama, would I live with you?"

"Baby, you will have a house of your own, a beautiful house overlooking the sea where you'll manage it wonderfully as I taught you. But you can visit me whenever you want, baby, this will still be your home and you're always welcomed here."

"Will you come see me?"

"Of course I will. The days that you can't come to me, I will make sure that I come instead."

I wanted to talk more, as if it was our last time to talk. I wanted to run and bury my face in her breasts and feel her warmth for the last time. I wanted to say that I want to stay with her forever, but I couldn't do any of that. I stood there numb, unable to react to the news, and saw her heavy body coming towards me. She stood there with tearful eyes and kissed my forehead. And we hugged; it was as if we'd never hug again. She held me tight and I didn't want to let go. When we finally left each other, I heard Mama's footsteps as she walked towards the door, and the moment she opened it, I heard the women in a cheerful scream announcing the start of the ceremony.

I could see Layla on the floor with my toys. She was calling me to play, but I didn't know how to tell her. I couldn't lose her, I couldn't lose her friendship. She was a beautiful little doll with long braided hair made of wool, and her stuffed body was tiny and fragile. Her dress was made of flowery cotton and her slippers were no more than a piece of cheap leather. She might have been just pieces of rags to everyone else, but to me she was the most wonderful and faithful friend in the whole world.

"I am getting married," I whispered into her invisible ears, "we don't have to play grown-ups any more, because we will be grown-ups."

"Will I, too?" said her still eyes.

"Yes of course. We will get all kinds of new toys to play with, even real cups for our tea parties. We will get to do all the stuff Mama taught us to do all on our own."

"But who are you marrying?"

"Well, let's not think about that as of yet, let's just think of all the gifts we will be getting and the new stuff. It will be fun. Mama says we will be celebrating the whole week. Let's start the ceremony."

I carried her and rushed to my room, not knowing if I actually meant what I said, or if I was trying to make myself feel better through my own words. Mama was already busy and she already looked happy, but I was scared.

The ceremony was to last all week. Every day marked a special theme. The first night, which took place on the same day I was told, was the announcement day. My mother dressed me in a beautiful turquoise dress, and I was showing off my elegant jewelry. I was wearing what we call the *gubgub* on my head, which looked like a bowl made of gold with many gold and precious stone extensions coming from it. My neck was decorated with the *mirta'asha*, long connected necklaces, and the *farasha*, which means butterfly in Arabic. The *farasha* was a huge necklace that took the shape of a butterfly designed with stones and diamond. It came with a bracelet set that was three inches wide and was connected with golden strings to the rings. Each finger had a ring but each was unique in style and stones. I also had a golden belt around my waist, again three inches wide, 24-carat gold. I had the anklets called *khulkhal* that Mama wore on her wedding and so was passed over to me, pure gold and silver with emerald and made a beautiful sound as I walked. My turquoise dress was of pure Indian silk embroidered in gold specially ordered from India, and I had a chiffon scarf on my head barely covering the *gubgub* and across my long, straight black hair. My aunts and neighbors spent all afternoon helping my mother as she started her daughter's *jihaz*, which was all the new things I got to take with me to my husband's house. My legs were waxed for the first time and the pain continued all day. The Moroccan bath was ticklish and the massage put me to sleep. So much happened that day and I enjoyed showing off my new things to my friends and the whole neighborhood or *fireej* was dancing and singing.

The second day was the *jihaz* day. It was like a fashion show where I got to try on everything new. I had so many *thoubs* or Arabian gowns brought to me and I had to see what fit and what needed fixing. That took all day as I tried underwear, *gub gab* or slippers, nightgowns, scarves etc. The whole neighborhood was welcomed to watch and cheer. Some were dancing and some were cooking for the fiesta to be held on the same night. When the evening prayers called out it was time to dress up for dinner. Mama had a red *thoub* waiting for me, again with pure silk and embroidery. She helped me put on my jewelry again and gave me her very own slippers. She combed my hair and walked with me to the guest section where I heard many *aaaahs* and *oooohs* as I walked in. The *sufra* or floor mat, which they put the food on, was even bigger tonight and I took my seat between my friends. The food was delicious and the scent of brewing Arabian coffee was luscious. As I was watching Mama from a distance, I could not help noticing how she looked happy and proud. She was sitting in the center of the room surrounded with her guests. She held her head straight up and carried a dignified smile. She was amazing. She was really something in our neighborhood. Every woman wanted to be her friend and every woman wanted to be her. She had an exquisite power and her words were truly respected. It's no wonder why our house was so crowded, everyone wanted to share Mama's joy. Everyone believed she deserved to feel blissful and hear her laughter echoing all over Bahrain. I was happier for her than I was for myself. I wanted to see her happy forever and I'd do whatever it would take to see that.

Day three was not any different. The invitations were to go out to everyone, but in my days there were no cards or so. The girls of my age would dress up in their best *thoubs* and gather in our house where my mother would give them directions to all the houses they would have to visit. In my wedding, which everyone was invited to, the girls would go from door to door singing to each an invitation song. I won't be surprised if Mama had invited all of Bahrain, for when the girls returned they looked dead tired, with hardly a breath left. The dress for that same night was yellow silk and silver embroidery. Mama left me to do my own make up, so I'd learn, and she only supervised. The same things continued, the dancing and the singing and the humungous dinner.

Day four was receiving the gifts from the husband's family. I hadn't met them yet and Mama said I would meet them all, including my husband, on my wedding day. I woke up filled with excitement as I couldn't wait to see the gifts, but Mama said that on this day I would have to dress up early, for everyone would be here to see the things. I took a long bath, had something to eat quickly and put on my pink *thoub* that had a golden scarf, and Mama helped me with my jewelry. My hands were shaking as I applied my make-up, so my Aunt Salwa helped me with the details. Then Mama accompanied me to the guest room where there was a big chair in the center decorated with flowers, and I was asked to sit there until the things arrived. The room soon was crowded with people and the heat was unbearable. I was starting to get really impatient when all of a sudden I heard the drums beat and the cheering of women and children. After a while, the door of the room opened and six big women were carrying big silver trays on their heads, and brought them in as they sang and danced at the same time. It seemed like these women were moving forever, each second passed like an hour, and all I could think of were my gifts. Finally, and after waiting forever, the ladies lowered the trays and as directed by Mama, placed them in order, right in front of me. The entire crowd gathered around me and I felt suffocated until my mother came to my rescue. She gave more space by allowing me to stand up, and with a wave from her elegant hands, the ladies started their second performance. The first walked to her tray. She lifted the velvet cloth gracefully to show the first group of gifts. I opened my eyes so wide, as if in fear of missing something, while the whisper of excitement echoed around me. It had two *sujadhhs*, or the rug we use specially for praying. This *sujadhh* though was pure Persian silk, decorated in flowers and leaves. It also had the *sharshaf*, which is what we cover our heads with, and that was made of pure silk as well. The *subha*, or praying beads, were made of emerald, and there was a Quran too inside an emerald and gold box. As the lady took this tray to show the guests, the second tray was brought. This tray consisted of elegant textiles, all embroidered in gold and silver. Some were silk, some were chiffon, and some were both, all in different royal colors. The third gift was two pairs of slippers, one was in brown leather and gold, and the other was black and silver. I never got to wear them in all the years I had them, they were way too heavy to walk in. The fourth tray had a silver comb set with matching mirror. It also had a matching make up set with brushes and a hairbrush. It had silver incense bottles and a silver box filled with incense powder. The fifth tray carried a vast *mubkhara*, which is a stand with an opened circle top with a deep hole used for burning incense. The *mubkhara* was handmade silver decorated with emerald. The last, but definitely not least, was the most important. It was my dowry made of an emerald ten-inch box filled with gold and silver coins. More gold coins were also put in small green velvet patches placed all around the big box. The lady carrying the box didn't seem pleased though as the poor thing was stuck with the heaviest tray. This was certainly my favorite day.

Day five was a relaxing day for me. I didn't have anything to do but rest and play with my friends. That's because on this day, Mama had to invite my husband's family for lunch and dinner, but I was not to be seen yet. I was glad that I could at least have one more day with my friends before I bid my childhood farewell.

Day six was the henna night. I was dressed in green and sat in the middle of the *housh*. My mama's friend was designing a beautiful pattern with henna on my feet and hands that was really ticklish but nice at the same time. All my friends got to put on henna as well. That was a must in my days, the henna before the wedding. Men liked it back then; it was a sign of beauty. The poor had it on in occasions and the rich adorned themselves with it all the time. The whole house was decorated in green as well. I never knew why the color green had to be used on henna night, but it was a universal thing. The whole house smelt of *mashmoum*, a strong scented plant, and Mama had a professional singer come for the occasion.

Mama looked extra beautiful today. Her long hair was braided neatly to the back and tied with a brooch covered in precious stones that Baba had given her as a gift. Her green gown was flowing on her smooth skin and her scarf added to her grace. She wore a welcoming smile on her face and her eyes gave an extraordinary twinkle. This was to be my last night with her in this house. I couldn't even think about it. Mama and I had never been parted since I was born and now I was forced to leave when she needed me most. Our eyes finally met as we stared at each other from a distance. She blew me a kiss as she danced in a benign style, attracting everyone's attention.

The night passed so smoothly as I was carried to my room, unable to move from the henna in my feet and hands. I looked around in silence, staring at the empty walls, as all my belongings had now been packed. The brown leather bags lay in front of my eyes waiting to be carried to my new home. My new home. I wondered what it would look like. Would it have a private well or would I have to walk to a nearby well. Would I have a *housh*? Would my friends still be able to visit me? Would it be far away from Mama? What would my husband be like? Was he handsome? Was he like my Baba? Would he be good to me?

Too many questions were on my mind but all of a sudden my eyes were set on the corner of my room where Layla sat ignored. I wanted to hold her but she seemed so far away. Layla was already angry with me.

"Don't be angry, sweet Layla. I know I have been too busy to even hold you, but I promise it will only get better," I told her.

"I have lost you forever," she said.

"We will never lose each other, I promise you that. We will be together to share our secrets and share our laughter. No one will replace you no matter what."

But she knew things were changing. Though I was clinging on to the past she saw it clearly that our friendship could not be as it was. I already didn't have time to play with her and I wasn't even married yet.

"What are you doing awake at this time?" Mama surprised me, "you are the bride, baby. Would we want tired eyes for our beautiful bride?"

"I can't sleep, Mama. I can't stop thinking that this is my last night here."

"It might be the end of one life but the start of another, a more exciting one," she whispered, as if trying to convince herself before trying to convince me.

"Khadeeja, I am actually glad you didn't sleep, I have been so busy with the arrangements that we hardly even spoke to each other. Baby, there are things you need to know about marriage things you might not have heard about before." And Mama went on explaining all the details of marriage, and my God they were too many things I didn't know. Getting married was not as easy as I thought it was and I was starting to get scared. Mama tried to describe things clearly; some of my questions she was willing to answer, others she had a difficult time answering, but it was a talk I would never forget.

"Don't be afraid, Khadeeja, every woman goes through her wedding night and every woman had to face this experience," she told me.

"Is he going to hurt me, Mama, will I be in pain?"

"Only at first but don't think about the pain, think about the beautiful life that is waiting for you. Think of your future."

"But why do I have to go through this?"

"You will understand later, you will know the answer after you become a woman. Khadeeja, when you give yourself to your husband and he gives you himself you will create a passionate, intimate relationship that will go on forever. You will want each other, you will love each other, and this love will only grow with time."

"How did you feel, Mama, that night, the night you first met Baba?"

"My mama didn't tell me anything about marriage and the first night and love. Abdullah, your father, walked into the bedroom after the wedding ceremony as I hid myself under the black *abaya*," Mama laid next to me as she smiled back at the flowing memories. "He was young, shy and handsome. I was shaking but as he sat next to me to lift my *abaya* so he'd see his bride, I fell in love with him at that very instant. I saw him get ready to sleep and so I did the same not knowing what was yet to come. It was Allah's strength that made me go through the first night."

"Were you afraid of him?"

"I was at first but as the night went by I realized that he didn't mean to hurt me. His touch was kind and loving. His smile was comforting. And I gave him myself, all I had, all that was precious. He owned me but he also made sure that I owned him too."

"Did you love him?"

"More than anything in the world. I still do, you know. Whenever I close my eyes I see him there standing right in front of me, tall, handsome, with his dignified smile and deep eyes. My heart would skip beats and my body would shiver, aching for his touch. But then I realize he is only a dream, he is not there any more, and I would cry for him all over again."

"I wish I'd met him."

"I wish you had. I know he would've loved you as much as I do. I am sure he does anyway. I am sure he is watching us right now, laughing at what we are saying and happy for his daughter. Oh Khadeeja, look at you, all ready to leave your mama's arms."

"Do I have to? Do I have to get married now?"

"It's what's best for you. You might not think so now but someday you will understand." And she kissed my forehead.

Mama was so calm, so beautiful, so understanding. It was like we were on a planet of our own, no one to bother us, no one to take me away from her. She would hold my hand at times and brush my hair at others. She would smile in shyness or laugh in impishness. Never had we such moments before and never did we have it again, for as she sat singing me to sleep for the last time we were both bidding my childhood farewell forever.

★

Day seven was the final night. It was Thursday early morning when Mama woke me up for a breakfast buffet. I woke up confused, as if in a terrible dream but the day was so clear and the breeze was so cool that my confusion soon was replaced by a cheerful mood. After the wonderful breakfast of fresh *khubis khabaz*, *balaleet* (sweet noodles with eggs), *mihyawa* (sour salty sauce), *baloo* (like *mihyawa* but powder) and assorted cheese and fruit I was off to my Moroccan bath and massage. I was so tense that the massage wasn't as enjoyable this time, but Mama was with me to calm me down with her soothing words. I was then covered in scented oil from head to toe while waiting for my quick lunch. Mama then took me into a different room, her own room, where I would be applying my make-up. Mama and Aunt Jameela decided I shouldn't hide my natural beauty with make-up and so I used a little powder with some *kihil*, eyeliner, and lipstick would be enough. Mama then combed my hair and pulled it back in a pony tail, then covered most of it with the jasmine flower that matched perfectly with my white, silver and gold dress. My jewelry made a funny noise as I was shivering and my *khulkhal* felt too heavy on my feet. Mama slipped a small Quran in my right pocket, and as I made sure I was totally ready I heard the start of the drums, singing and clapping that marked the start of the final ceremony. Mama left me to welcome the guests and I was surrounded with my astonished friends and cousins who were either checking the fabric of my dress, or placing more jasmine into my hair or making sure the jewelry was correctly placed. And finally Mama walked in with my veil made of silver and gold threads. As she placed it on my face she kissed my forehead, and held my hand so tightly leading me to the reception hall. I was so terribly shy while walking down the *housh* between the people that I felt a faint, but Mama's hand and proud walk rescued me from embarrassing myself. The dress was too heavy and I hardly noticed any one. It was loud, hot and crowded and I wished I had Layla with me. My stomach wouldn't stop making noises as I saw the ladies eat while I had to wait to eat with my husband. I took quick glances at my mother-in-law who seemed kind. His sisters were old, much older than I, and they all had a funny expression on their faces. Mama later on told me they were impressed with my beauty and paid the matchmaker double her price. I could tell that some of the guests were happy for me and some had envious looks, but all that really mattered at that moment was food, I really was hungry.

And finally it was time to go.

Mama walked towards me but I couldn't help realizing how heavy each step seemed and how sad her face looked. At that moment I wanted the ground below me to open up and swallow me. I wanted to run to my room and lock the door behind me but I stood there paralyzed and in total bewilderment.

"Baby, are you ready?"

"Mama, I don't want to go. Please let me spend another night with you."

"Khadeeja we already talked about it. Really it isn't as bad as you think it is. Come on, baby, your husband is waiting for you, don't you want to start a new life? Come on, baby, you will be a happy, good wife."

And slowly I walked towards my room to wear my *abaya*, the black overgarment we wear over our clothing before we go out. As I opened the heavy wooden door that somehow felt heavier, I saw a rather sad face staring at me. Layla was thrown where I last saw her but I felt her eyes towards me, screaming to be held. I ran to her, hugged her so tightly, knowing that she was my last link to my childhood. I took a very last look around my room; how cold and empty it felt. I lived every single minute of my life between these walls. These floors marked my first footsteps, these walls had my name carved on them, these windows brought so much brightness into my days, this is my home and home is where the heart is.

I heard Mama's call from behind the door as I put on my *abaya* at a snail's pace. Layla was still in my hands and I could not let go. Mama's voice grew louder and I was in the middle of a dilemma and finally decided to hide her under the dress as I walked out.

"Khadeeja, dear, we are late. What is that you have under your dress?"

I could never hide a thing from Mama, it was like she knew me too well.

"It's Layla, Mama, I can't leave without her."

"Khadeeja, you can't possibly go to your husband's house with a doll."

"But you don't understand, this is my best friend. Please Mama, I promise he won't see it."

It was like I was fighting for my past, my childhood, things I didn't want to give up, not yet. I didn't know if Mama would ever understand me or know what Layla meant to me but her eyes said a lot. It was like Mama was starting to regret her decision and feel sorry for me, and I longed for a word that would make me stay with her.

"I promise you, Khadeeja, that I will send you Layla first thing tomorrow."

I watched her as Mama carried her away and my heart ached. I knew she was crying, she had always been frightened of the dark and I had to leave her in the dark. She was frightened of sleeping alone and I had to leave her to sleep alone. I was a bad friend and my Layla would never forgive me for it.

Feeling defeated I set off towards the outside door with all my relatives behind me with lanterns, and walked towards my new home. The ladies were singing and clapping but I could hardly hear a sound. My mind went blank and I could hardly walk. My heart skipped beats and I could barely breathe. I wanted to run back home but Mama's hand held me firmly as she walked with dignity beside me. Usually it was the husband who would come to the bride but Mama had insisted that the wedding take place in her house and she would take me herself to my new home. My eyes were filled with tears as I saw the decorated house ahead. I suddenly realized I didn't even know my husband's name.

"Mama, what's his name?" I whispered.

Mama gave out a teasing laugh, "Mohammed," she said.

Mohammed. I was now Mrs. Mohammed. Was it really going to be good? Would my new life be adventurous and fun? Would he be good to me?

The house was big with beautifully carved wooden windows. The entrance had two tall palm trees and the steps stood as firm as a mountain beneath my feet. The air smelled of dates that hung on the trees waiting to be picked. The door was carved with flower and leaf shapes and had a big metal knob that was probably brought from India. Mama gave a gentle knock, opened the door slightly, turned me around and gave me a kiss on my forehead.

"Take care of yourself. Don't be afraid. I know for sure that you will be happy, baby. Be good to your husband, obey him. Do all that pleases him and so he'll do the same. Remember, Khadeeja, all that I taught you and remember that I will always be here for you."

And she pushed me in through the door, into a new life, a mysterious beginning and a baffling adventure. I longed for Layla; I longed for my home, my bedroom. Bang, the door shut behind me announcing that I was now alone. Mama was not there to protect me, I could not hide behind her any more. This was probably the most difficult moment of my life and there was no turning back. I could hear the women's slippers as they walked away, probably to Mama's house or to their own husbands' but I couldn't move. The *housh* seemed spacious and I could hardly see a thing. There was a lantern at the end of the fence showing some shadows that I guessed were doors. I was not used to wearing the *abaya*, which made it even harder to see. Was I alone here? I didn't know until I heard a whisper.

"Aren't you going to come in?" said a masculine voice in a rather shy tone.

"I didn't know which way to go," I said, unable to lift my eyes from the floor.

I heard footsteps coming towards me, heavy yet light at the same time. I could nearly hear my heartbeat and I felt my body sweat. I wished I could run away as far as I could and again I wished for Layla.

And then came the first touch. He left his hand resting on mine as he led me to the room. I didn't know what to feel, I was scared, I was shy, but mostly I was curious. I wanted to know who was the man holding my hand, what did he look like and what would my life with him be like. His touch was warm, his voice was sweet, and I could already feel his good vibe.

In no time I found myself in a pastel colored room. The lantern gave it a romantic touch and the jasmine gave it a cozy aroma.

"Would you like to give me your *abaya*," he said.

My *abaya*. Was I going to take it off in front of him? I was too shy with the thought of it. I was shy to meet him face to face but I was left with no choice. I felt his eyes studying me as I slowly managed to take it off with shivering hands. His hands touched my face as he slowly lifted it to lay his first looks and I was literally melting.

"You are more beautiful than I thought," he said softly.

"Thank you," I said, unable to think of anything else.

"Would you like to sit inside or do you prefer the *housh*? It's a wonderful night, the stars seem to be celebrating our new life and the breeze whispers the news of a bright future."

He seemed gentle and his words were sweet. He was very handsome, I could tell after stealing a quick look, and he tried to ease me up very smoothly. We sat to chat in the room for many hours until he left me to change my clothes. He was really tender, never pushed me or rushed me into anything, but gave me all the time I needed. I knew he was outside the bedroom door waiting for me, but I was scared. I remembered Mama's words and I knew he wasn't going to hurt me but I was shy, I just couldn't think of what was about to happen.

As I opened the door, he walked in slowly. I felt every step he took towards me. Though he was only a stranger a moment ago it suddenly didn't feel that way any more. He looked into my eyes and I felt him see through me, my soul, my life. At that moment I realized that I wasn't a child any more. I was in love, the way Mama fell in love with Baba. My heartbeat was racing time as he held me close to him. I was shy, I was shivering, but I also wanted him to take me. I wanted to get over the painful moment and feel true love. I wanted to start my new life. I had already bid my childhood farewell, I wanted to feel the passion, the affection, the love. I wanted to feel his care, his touch, his warmth.

He looked at me, and I knew it was all going to be okay. The pain was gone, the shiver was gone, I was still shy but I was fine. I was a woman.

He held me close, as I used to hold Layla, and fell asleep and I lay there wondering and giggling to myself. All of a sudden Mama's words now made sense. I felt good. I was welcoming my new life with optimism but I couldn't wait to see Layla.

Chapter Two

It was after noon when I first opened my eyes. Mohammed was still asleep. I had a headache and my body was aching from a long week of celebration. I couldn't believe it was over. I was too attached to the blanket; I didn't want to wake up but the breakfast had to be ready before Mohammed woke up. I was too shy to even look at him; I just couldn't believe I was a woman.

It felt funny. Only yesterday I was a little girl playing and running around the house with my friends and today I am a woman, I belong to a man, a handsome man. I opened my eyes for the first time in my life in a different house; I had never before left my mother's house, the house I was born in. My body felt different. It was touched by someone who was a stranger a moment ago and the closest man to me a moment later. Suddenly it was not mine any more. As eccentric as it all was, yet it felt so good.

After a quick bath I went to tour what everyone called my new house, funny for I am only a stranger in it. I dressed up in my baby blue gown, one of those I couldn't wait to wear from my *jihaz*. I combed my hair very quickly and rushed out the door to begin my adventure.

My room fell on the west side of the house. It was a perfect location to enjoy the morning sunlight and the evening breeze. It was the biggest room with two large windows, one overlooking the *housh* and the other overlooking the *bustan*, a garden of palm trees, and you could also see the sea from a distance. Next to my room was a smaller bedroom that had one window overlooking the *housh*. It was not furnished yet but it had a beautifully decorated ceiling. The kitchen was the largest I ever saw in my life. It was also one of the first kitchens in Bahrain to have a refrigerator: that made many envy me, and the wooden shelves were neatly packed with pots, pans, utensils, spices etc. The guest room or main living room was spacious, but not as spacious as my bedroom. The *doushag* and *misnad* (a thin mattress-like base to sit on and cushions) surrounded the room and the *sindoug embayat* (a carved wooden box with golden pins) stood proudly in a corner holding the dates and *qahwa* (coffee). The walls were decorated with colorful mirrored balls, picture frames with quranic verses, and sa'af (palm tree stems). Wooden pillars, called danchal, stretched through the ceiling and were painted in red, and the floor was covered with a colorful, thin straw mat. There were three windows; two small ones overlooking the garden and one towards the *housh*. The window panels carried glass vases, some decorated with flowers, some had *mashmoum* (a scented plant) in them. There was another living room, a smaller one that was probably for everyday use. The ceiling and floor were similar to that of the guest living room but the seating arrangement was different. The *doushag* and *misnad* were placed in one side of the room and the other side was a small *sindoug embayat* with a radio on top. There was a big basket made of palm tree leaves filled with *sijada* or praying rugs. There was a wooden shelf holding a bunch of fans which were also made of palm tree leaves that were very handy on hot, humid days, and right below it was a wooden stand holding a clay jar and some tin cups. There was a window overlooking the *housh* and some mirrors decorating the wall. The room in the eastern corner was the bathroom. It had a *tasht* or big metal bucket and two big cups used for the bath. There was the homemade soap that was also used as a shampoo and a comb on a small shelf. The window was close to the ceiling, yet not too high up, for privacy, and just big enough for some light. There was a wooden stool that was probably there for the lantern at night times. By the end of the wall was the servant's room. I didn't have servants yet but it was designed to be there for future use. That of course was not furnished. Last but not least there was the wooden entrance that reminded me of last night and my first steps into my home.

There was hardly any time left before Mohammed woke up so I hurried in to the kitchen and started fixing the first meal of my new life. I managed to find the ingredients for the bread dough and in case I forgot to mention, I did have my own *tanoor*, or brick oven in the *housh*. I made some eggs; cut some white cheese, some olives, some *za'atar* and some *mihyawa*. I made some *balaleet* and after deciding to have breakfast while enjoying the beautiful weather in the *housh* I placed everything on the *sufra* and started baking my bread.

"Wow, that smells good," Mohammed surprised me.

"Let's hope it tastes good. I still have a lot to learn. Would you like to drink some tea while I bake the bread?"

"Yes, that is a good idea."

I ran as quickly as I could to put some water on the fire before I burned any bread, but when I came back Mohammed had taken over the baking."

"You shouldn't have had done all of this you are still a bride," he said.

"I woke up and found you still asleep so I thought of surprising you."

"That was very nice of you, thank you." And I knew I had impressed him. I could feel the butterflies in my stomach as I turned my shy face away, hiding its redness, and I couldn't wait to tell my Layla all this. She would be happy for me and who knows, maybe even jealous.

Was I the princess who had just found her prince and the promise of eternal love? Was my life suddenly a page from a fairy tale book? It was beautiful. Never had I felt that way before. If only my father was alive, if only he had lived to see this day. I looked up at the blue sky, wondering if my Baba was watching me, wondering if he was proud of what he saw, if he was happy. And if he couldn't see me I wished from all my heart that the angels would tell him all about this day, about my joy and ecstasy and how I longed for his presence among us. May he rest in peace.

After breakfast Mama came to visit and so did my aunts. I really missed Layla but Mama couldn't bring her along for she came with Mohammed's family, which I hadn't met personally yet.

Mohammed's family, Alkooky, lived in Persia. His great grandfather, who was a scholar, went to Persia to start a Quran school that soon became well known. Being religiously educated made him the sheikh for his town and so he decided to stay in Persia. Mohammed's father, Aqeel, was also a religious sheikh after his own father, and his mother was a nearby town sheikh's daughter. Mohammed was the radical one in the family. He did not want to stay all his life in a religious institution, but traveled around to learn medicine. He soon became a qualified nurse and found a job in Bahrain's only hospital. A qualified nurse in Bahrain was a rare thing and so Mohammed was considered as a doctor and therefore treated as a royal in the society. Once he had built a home and settled he decided to marry, and upon hearing that his desperate mother and sisters came from Persia to start the matchmaking.

Khariya was our neighborhood matchmaker. She arranged all my aunts' marriages and even my parents' marriage. Mama told me once that before Baba went to India, his last trip, he called for Khariya and paid her well. "You are to find a good husband for my child if Aisha happened to have a baby girl, bring her a good man, a man who fears God, from a good family, and a good reputation. A hard-working man who would make her live the way I would," he told her. When Khariya knew about the Alkooky's search for a bride I was the first to come to mind. We had the same background and she believed I had all they were looking for. We were both from well-off families, we were both from the same class, we were both Sunnis and our grandparents were both religious leaders. I had all the beauty, reputation, smartness, manners and character they were looking for, and he was rich so she knew he'd pay her good money.

Mama believed he was a good man from what she had heard about him. She alone was hoping for a good match, after knowing about her fatal illness, and after making sure he was what my father would have chosen himself, if he'd been alive, she agreed on the proposal.

Khariya talked so much about me and my family that the Alkookys started the marriage arrangement before even meeting me, and the wedding came soon after.

Now that their son had settled and they were impressed with the matchmaking, my mother-in-law and sisters-in-law had to take off back to Persia, and so I would have to meet them one last time before they left.

★

Mohammed left for work and the house was soon packed with people. I was too tired to see anyone but people kept on coming endlessly, and Mama and Aunt Jameela played the host. My mother-in-law, Yuma Amina, was sitting next to me and I could tell my sisters-in-law were already feeling envious. She had brought along a gift from Persia, a set of bangles, and helped me put them on with the promise to show Mohammed when he returned. She seemed nice, a very old woman much older than Mama. Her hair was orange, probably from henna, and her skin was wrinkled yet soft and white. She was a neat woman, elegant for her age, and always wore all her jewelry, "even when she sleeps," Khariya told me.

Mohammed's sisters-in-law, his brothers' wives, were not pleased with what they saw. Though I was twelve years old I could still understand such things. They were protesting against the fact that I would live in a house of my own and they, though much older than I, still lived with Yuma Amina. Well, I guess I was lucky on that one, because newlyweds usually stayed at their in-laws, especially in Persia, during the first couple of years, until they could have a place of their own. But my in-laws lived thousands of miles away, and living with Mama wasn't going to be comfortable for Mohammed because it was kind of far from the hospital. I was even told that Mohammed wouldn't allow it even if we were in Persia. He was open-minded and always wanted his independence; living with his family would have suffocated him. And after the last night's talk I could figure out that he never wanted to return to Persia. I hated this gossiping and the looks of anger but I was glad they were leaving soon. I believed I was privileged not because I owned my house but because I wouldn't be living with such pressure. I was hoping they were closer to my age so I could play with them but they were grown women and I was only a child.

Just after sunset the house was finally quiet with only Mama and Yuma Amina left. I wished I could have some time alone with Mama and I knew she felt the same way but she had to leave before dark. As I bid them farewell I saw Mohammed's shadow walking towards us.

"Asalam aleikum, how are you Yuma Aisha, how are you Mother?" he screamed.

"Good, my son, good," said Mama, "and you? You seem awfully tired for a new husband."

"What can I say? It's like the hospital was punishing me for getting married. I had a neverending line of patients all for vaccinations," he said with a smile.

"I am sure Khadeeja will make you forget all that you've been through." Yuma Amina said naughtily.

"Where are you going, why don't you stay for dinner?" he asked them as he looked at me, hoping that they'd turn him down.

"No, no, you kids go ahead. Amina will be having dinner in my house tonight. It's getting dark we should hurry," said Mama, trying to pull Yuma Amina with her.

"Yes, yes, bye bye now," she answered back.

As they left Mohammed gave me a kiss on my forehead and we stood side by side, watching them go into the darkness. It was ticklish feeling his masculine hands on my waist. It was deep, very warm, I wished I could tell him not to remove them; let them be as they are forever. He pulled me into the house and hugged me so tight while he closed the door and started teasing me as I lowered my red face in shyness.

I was a child experiencing her first encounter with a man, a stranger yet someone who stirred an unknown feeling in my heart. Mohammed was able to fall in love with me in a very short time. I was a child but I was smart, I was intelligent and I tried to keep up with his level of knowledge though I was illiterate. I was curious, always asking him about the books he was reading, and he enjoyed sharing his insights with me. It made us closer, friends and lovers, student and teacher.

"I am so hungry, I had no time to even have a bite today," he said, walking towards the living room.

"Give me a minute and I will have dinner ready," I said hurriedly and walked into the kitchen to find dinner waiting for us. I was sure Mama had prepared this knowing that I was too busy with guests to cook.

We sat down to eat and he started talking about his day. He began doing imitations and I couldn't stop laughing. He was funny, he always stayed that way. He came into the kitchen with me, washed the plates as well and helped me put things where they belong. That was definitely something unusual, for it was well known that such things were a woman's job, but Mohammed was different. He was open, understanding and truly unique. I believed my life would be heaven with him, I really did. I never complained about him the way others complained about their husbands. The days only brought us closer to each other and it was friendship that built our relationship. He was honest, kind and moderate, always ready with a nice word. His compliments made me want to give him more and his adoring looks made me the happiest women alive.

That was our life, simple, joyful and exciting. When he left for work I would count the seconds till he was back and when he was back I'd run into his arms as I would run to welcome Baba if he were alive. It was beautiful the feelings I had for him were breathtaking, and something I never felt before towards anyone, not even Mama or even Layla. I think it was what everyone called love, something I thought I'd only hear or know about in love stories.

★

The first time I went to see Mama was an unforgettable visit. Walking in my old *fireej* felt weird. My childhood was screaming from everywhere and I almost felt like I was coming back from a different planet. There was *eldukkan*, or mini market. Wow Shammad, the market's old man, seemed older and how differently he treated me now, as he would Mama, as if I wasn't that little girl who ran to him to bye some candy just yesterday. Ahead of me was the *qahwa*, coffee shop; Abbass used to invite me and my friends for some juice, now he hardly looked towards me. Banat *elfireej*, or neighborhood girls, were still playing as I left them. I wished I could throw my *abaya* and run to them but that would be a disaster, a married woman playing? Unheard of. I could see the women turning towards me, I could almost hear their whisper, "there goes the lucky one, what a catch, who wouldn't want to be the wife of a doctor."

And there it was, my home, my childhood, my memories, the most beautiful days of my life. The door seemed to call me from a distance, the windows appeared to be clapping for my return, and the palm trees were dancing, announcing my arrival as the birds sang in joy. I longed for my return. I longed for Mama, for Layla, for my room, even Zin Khaloy, and Ismat, our servants. Mama had always taught me to knock the door as a delicate lady, but at such a moment I couldn't control myself. I ran, embraced the door and banged like an attacking animal. Zin Khaloy was the first to see me and she let out a joyful scream that brought everyone to the door. Mama was of course in tears and everyone else hugged and kissed me as if I had been away for a very long time. Mama held my hand tightly and took me towards her room where she helped me take my *abaya* off and offered a fan, for the weather was very hot and humid and my house was far.

"Tell me, sweet daughter, is Mohammed a good man? Has he been good to you? Have you been good to him? Where is he? Why hasn't he come with you?"

"Yes Mama, he is a very good man. Baba would have loved him if he was alive, he would have been like a son to him. He is kind and funny. You know, Mama, he even comes into the kitchen to help me."

"That is good, Khadeeja, I am happy for you. Now I can rest in peace knowing that you are in safe hands. Tell me are you comfortable with your new life?"

"Yes, Mama, I am. I know now that my life will be good."

"Where is Mohammed? I have missed him."

"Mohammed is really busy these days. Many people are planning for a pilgrimage to Mecca, so medical check ups have filled his time. He told me that he won't be back before *maghreb*, sunset, so I took permission to come see you."

"Good, baby. So you'll have lunch with us then?"

"I guess so. It's too hot to walk back in the afternoon."

And I watched Mama as she struggled to lift her heavy body from the floor. A hand was on her lower back and another on her knee, she seemed in pain as I rushed to help her, but she said she was just fine, didn't need my help, believing that depending on her self was a good exercise.

As she went into the kitchen to see if lunch was ready I walked slowly towards my room. I didn't know why it was so difficult to see my room, to see Layla, and I felt numb. As I opened the door to the empty room all my memories came back to me with the fragrance of the cracked walls. It seemed so dark; the window shutters were shut yet the light seemed to sneak through between the wooden panes. The carpet was not there any more and the doors of the closet were wide open.

My eyes were studying my room; my heart was searching for Layla. And there she was, sitting in the closet, looking towards the door as if waiting for the moment of my return. I rushed to pick her up and hugged her so tight I thought I'd tear her apart, yet somehow I felt her hugging back. She was as beautiful as I saw her last, yet in a way seemed sad. I cried. I cried for leaving her, I cried for being unable to play with her as I used to. I cried for being unable to take her with me to my new home, show her where I live, and I cried for having to share only memories with her. I didn't want to let go. I knew Mohammed would understand but it was society that did not allow me to keep my last childhood remembrance.

I saw Mama's shadow as she walked in with a smile of empathy as she held both Layla and me in her arms.

"Every woman goes into such a transition, Khadeeja. You just have to learn to accept it."

"But Mama, I miss you, my home, my room. Why can't Mohammed come live with us?"

"No, Khadeeja, no husband is comfortable in a place other than his own house. Let me tell you something. You can take Layla with you today on one condition."

"Oh anything, Mama, I would do anything."

"You don't get to play with her when Mohammed or anyone else is home."

I felt my heart jump with happiness. My day was bright again and I loved Mama even more.

"Thank you, thank you, thank you! I can't thank you enough! I love you, Mama, I love you."

"Do you? Do you, baby? Do you really love me?"

I looked into her tearful eyes that ached to hear the words of love. I saw the memories of Baba coming back as she cried and I saw the pain and suffering of being alone reborn all over again. I forgot all about Layla, threw her aside and went into my mama's arms.

"Do you have any doubt that you are the most important person in my life? That I will love no one the way I love you, that I will look up to no one but you, that I am grateful for the countless sacrifices you have made to see me happy, that I will cherish all that I have learned from you? Do you have any doubt that you are inside me every second, that your smile is the first that comes to mind when I wake up and go to sleep? Oh Mama, you mean the world to me. I can never love you enough and no words could ever describe how I truly feel."

And we sobbed. We held each other so tight as if in fear of losing each other. For the first time in my life I saw the great Mama broken into pieces in front of me. It was a scene I would never forget.

Ismat walked in to call us for lunch, and finding us as we were she too got emotional, but tried to get herself together and calmed us down. Lunch was really delicious that day and I stayed with Mama until right before the *maghreb* prayer. Mama walked me to the door as I held Layla in my arms, we kissed and I promised I'd be back with Mohammed on Friday, our holy day.

Chapter Three

Mohammed woke me up at dawn one day as usual for the *fajr* prayer. I felt uneasy, heavy and drowsy at the same time. The minute I stood up I collapsed on the floor and Mohammed carried me back to the bed. He took my temperature, measured my pulse, but nothing seemed wrong. After completing his prayers he convinced me to go with him to the hospital and promised to walk with me back home. The worried look on his face made me give in to anything and it was good to feel so loved.

The sun was just starting to spread its rays and the men were busy with a new day. The hospital was close to the house and I could already see its huge gates. The aroma of medicine was nauseating and there wasn't enough light coming in. It wasn't as big as I had imagined it to be, just a little roomier than my house and Mama's put together. Mohammed took me into a room and asked me to stay there until he returned. The door was left open so I could see the lines of sick people forming and the courtyard was busy in no time. Finally he came in with an old man I guessed to be the doctor. He had a white beard, thick heavy glasses and an extra large white doctor coat. Mohammed didn't have one of those; he would wear a normal shirt and trousers, which was nicer of course. Mohammed was saying something to this doctor whom I believed needed a doctor himself. He walked towards me and somehow managed to speak a word, for he was very old.

"Aahh, how are you feeling now?"

"Good," I said in a fearful voice.

"Have you been throwing up?"

"No, but sometimes I feel like I want to."

I felt his heavy hand examining my belly and I thanked God Mohammed was still with me. Otherwise I think I might have started screaming.

After some examinations he said with a funny smile, "*mabrook mabrook* congratulations, you're pregnant."

Pregnant! Mohammed was jumping with joy and I was confused. I was happy; I was scared I didn't know what to do. Mohammed helped me off the bed and even made me walk as slow as a turtle. Wow, pregnant. That meant I had a little thing living inside me. I will become a real mother, just as I used to play with Layla. My tummy will soon get big and I will not be able to run any more, but that's okay, Layla will have a sister or brother to play with.

Mohammed was really happy. He couldn't believe that he was going to be a father, "I was waiting for it all my life," he shouted. "I will invite all the neighborhood, I will have a big party when the baby is born, my baby will carry my name," he kept on screaming as we walked back home. He took the rest of the day off and pampered me to the extent that I wished I could be pregnant forever. He was dancing at times, singing at times, and wouldn't let me move an inch. He was happy.

"What should we call him or her?" he asked.

"What would you prefer a boy or a girl?"

"Both. I want a boy and a girl, whatever God wants to give us. I pray for the baby's health, that is the most important thing."

"I am happy I heard that, I was scared you might be the kind of husband who only wants boys and would neglect the girls. Some friends told me it was a blessing not to have a father. Some of them didn't exist to their fathers just because they were girls. 'It's a man's world' they would say."

"What do you want? A girl or a boy?" he asked.

"I'd say exactly what you'd say, if it's a boy I'll teach him to be a man like you, and if it was a girl I'll enjoy having her around me as I was around Mama."

"And I would love you more for not only being my wife but the mother of my children too."

His words were so beautiful that I felt butterflies in my stomach. As I lowered my head in shyness he said, "Let's go tell your mother I'm sure she'll be very happy."

I jumped with the thought and ran to change my clothes as he screamed back, "be careful. You know you can't do that now."

I locked the door behind me and ran to tell Layla. I knew she would be as happy as I was, I knew she would jump on her feet and scream with laughter, only if she could.

"Did you hear that? You will have a sister or brother to play with, Layla."

"You will be a mama?" she whispered.

"We won't have to act like one when we're playing because I will be one now, a real one."

"Oh, it's so beautiful to be human. I wish I had a baby of my own."

"My baby is yours, you know that, and I will be depending on you a lot so you better prepare yourself."

And we sat there laughing at the whole thing. It seemed like yesterday where we would stuff our dresses with pillows to imitate pregnant women and now I am one of them. I wouldn't have to stuff my dress any more, I was pregnant and it felt so good to be pregnant.

*

It was a cloudy day. It was an unusual time for rain but this island was full of surprises. As Mohammed and I approached Mama's house I started imagining how I would tell her the news. Would I run and scream it out or would I let her guess what news I carried for her? Would I whisper it to her ears and give her the joy of announcing it to the world or would I let Mohammed do the honor? What would she do? Would she cry? Would she scream? Would she laugh? It was one of the times I wished Baba was alive. He would have been happy, I was sure of that.

The house door was in front of me but something unusual was going on. The door was open; our door was never open like that with no one there, no one coming in or out. As we got closer there was a cry, a whispering cry and another voice gasping for air. As Mohammed and I rushed in we realized it was Zin Khaloy and Ismat who only cried louder as soon as our eyes met.

"What? What? What is it? Where is Mama? What is the matter? What is going on? Someone say something, anything?"

"Oh baby, Khadeeja, how can we say a word," cried Zin Khaloy.

"Did something happen to Mama?"

"Oh what can I do, there was nothing I could do!" cried Ismat.

"Would you just say what happened?" said Mohammed impatiently.

"Doctor, she is lying in the room, she is not breathing, I don t know what to do."

Mama. Something was wrong with my mama. I felt numb; I was confused. Mohammed rushed into the bedroom and I could hardly take a step. Zin Khaloy held my hand so tightly and helped me walk in, and I wished I never had walked into that room on that day. Mohammed's face was pale as he looked at me and shook his head. Mama looked like an angel. Her heavy body looked so light and her skin seemed to glow. Her beauty hid her weakness yet sickness left its marks everywhere.

Mama had died that day before I even had the chance to say goodbye. Before knowing that I was pregnant, that she was to be a grandmother. At that moment I ached for a lullaby, her lullaby. I ached for her touch, her kiss, her soothing words and her warm arms. I ached for her voice, her eyes, her kindness and love. How can I live without my mama? How can I wake up with the thought that I won't see her today or ever again? How can I live without her watching over me, helping me, advising me? I want my mama. I never wanted her as much as I wanted her now, only for a last hug, only to be in my true home in her arms, only to kiss her forehead and hear her sing our last song.

There wasn't any time to grieve. The house was soon crowded with family and Mama was taken away. Her funeral was to be held that same day after the afternoon prayer, and then the house would remain crowded for the next three days for people who wanted to pay respect and give their condolences.

Aunty Jameela, the only one who knew I was pregnant at the time, held my hand as we walked towards the magbara, graveyard. Mohammed, Aziz, Hassan and some relative were carrying Mama, who was all in white, in her kafan. Aziz and Hassan had come to visit Mama only two days ago, as if knowing they had to see her one last time.

We read Alfatiha, a *soora* from the Quran, as Mama was being lowered slowly into her grave, and I could hear Aziz's voice as he cried in pain. Hassan looked faint and Mohammed was worried about me.

I sobbed like I have never sobbed before. A beautiful day ended up being the worst day of my life. I was an orphan now and I was scared. The next three days were difficult. People came and went but I wasn't able to grasp anything. Mama's memories were everywhere. I wanted to go home; I wanted Mohammed to comfort me. I wanted to deny the truth. I wanted Mama to walk in at that second and hold me close to her. Aunty Jameela would take me every now and then to go into my room and lay down. She was too concerned with me being pregnant and I had no idea about what to do and what not to do. Finally, I went home the third day. Mohammed came to pick me up and he looked tired himself.

I cried for hours in his lap and he was never as comforting as that day. He took a month off from work and stayed at home to nurse me and I needed it. I was tired, I was exhausted and depression took over me completely. Being pregnant only added to my distress as my morning sickness increased and I hardly had an appetite.

I grew attached to Mohammed even more. The feeling of losing someone precious made me scared, afraid of death, of the future, even of the little being inside me. I had gone through too much pain in losing Mama and I couldn't bear the thought of going through that pain again. I didn't want to lose Mohammed nor did I want to lose my child, and only Layla seemed to understand my fears.

Aziz and Hassan left just two days after Mama's funeral. They were both heading back to Dubai after trying to convince Mohammed to move there with them. The economy was booming and they believed it was their chance in the market. Mohammed, though, was happy in his job. He was promised many promotions and raises, for he was devoted to his work and thought to be one of the lucky ones. And so we stayed in our beloved Bahrain, a place I would never think of leaving anyway.

Layla was sad too but we couldn't talk, I was too tired to talk. I would only look at her from time to time, I would wink or smile to comfort her but I needed all the comfort in the world myself. It was a difficult time and I could not think of anything at all.

Chapter Four

"That was the most difficult time of my life," I said to Layla, not knowing what was yet to come. My first pregnancy was a smooth one as I had help from everyone. Aunty Jameela would stop by every now and then to check on me and Mohammed had hired a maid to take over house chores.

It was a kind of routine that I got myself into just to keep my mind busy and so not think of Mama and my loneliness. I would cook in the morning and then gather with my friends in the *bustan* until before *maghreb* when I would head back home to wait for Mohammed's return. We would then have our dinner followed by some tea, as he would enjoy his hubbly bubbly, or shisha.

Until one night after Mohammed had gone to sleep, I found myself in a pain so unbearable that I could not even get myself to lie down. I started walking in the *housh* as if in pilgrimage but the pain would continue to grow. After some time I realized it was time. I had to wake Mohammed up, and as I walked towards the room my water broke; not knowing what that was I let out a scream that I think woke the whole *fireej* up.

"What, what Khadeeja? Where are you?" screamed Mohammed, as he hardly saw a thing.

"My God, it's water, there is water everywhere!"

"What water, are you dreaming? Did you drop the water jar?"

"No, Mohammed, my water, water from me."

"Oh my God, you are in labor, why didn't you tell me?"

And I started to scream. There were contractions that came after each other with hardly any gaps between them. Mohammed managed to carry me inside and ran to bring the midwife even though he was prepared to deliver our child but he was too nervous to focus. *Alwallada* or midwife, was there in no time but I thought that death had taken over me. I wished Mama was here, she would have known how to calm me down. I wished I could hold Layla, for I knew her eyes would have encouraged me and her still face would remind me that everything would be alright. Why is it that every time you need something so bad it's so far away from you?

"Push, Khadeeja, push" was all I heard. I felt Aunty Jameela's hand holding me, not knowing how or when she came. I heard Mohammed's voice in prayer from outside as he pleaded with God for my safety and his child's, of course. I heard the maid running around the room in confusion and fear. I pushed so hard that I thought my soul would leave my skeleton. It was a struggle between life and death and I prayed for help until I heard Mama's voice deep in my heart whispering, "you can do it, baby, you can do it," and I heard the first cry. My baby was born.

I fought to catch my breath as I heard Aunty Jameela screaming, "It's a girl, Mohammed, it's a beautiful baby girl."

A girl. My eyes were searching for Layla to tell her the news. She had a sister to play with. A baby girl.

Aunty Jameela gave me my baby to hold for the first time as Mohammed came in. She looked so beautiful and tiny and fragile. She was all wrapped up in a white cloak, such a tiny thing, 2.4 kilos, but beautiful. I haven't seen anything more beautiful than that. Yes, she definitely had Mohammed's eyes, and her nose was so tiny you could hardly tell its shape. Her lips were my lips but more of a raspberry color. Her color was mine too, more tanned than yellow or white. Her hair was dark, not black but maybe dark brown. She looked so fragile and as I held her close to me she seemed to tuck herself in more and bury her head in my breasts. Her hand was like a little teddy bear's hand and her fingers were long, like those of an artist. Her skin was so soft that you couldn't help but caress it and as I heard her breathe I couldn't believe that it was me who brought this beauty into life.

"Wow, a baby girl, you gave me a baby girl," said Mohammed in tears.

"Isn't she the most beautiful thing?"

"Oh, she is, she is a miracle."

"What should we name her?"

"It was you who went through all that pain and throbbing, you should have the honor of naming her," he said.

As I looked at her I remembered Mama's voice telling me 'you could do it baby'. I remembered how she died the day I found out I was pregnant, how I believed she would be the happiest if she were alive, and in a way I felt her there with us, sharing the day with me. I believed it was she who helped me through the delivery and it was her warmth, her spirit, her love that filled the room. As I looked at my baby's eyes I saw Mama and I believed that this tiny thing was born with Mama's soul.

"Aisha," I said confidently. "I want to name her Aisha. I want to give her my mama's name so she grows to be like my mama, an amazing, wonderful, beautiful woman."

"Aisha, what a beautiful name," said Mohammed supporting my decision.

The sun was rising; the clouds had taken a beautiful shade of red and orange. I couldn't believe that I was a mother but I felt it. There was this new feeling inside me, very warm, very compassionate. It was a different kind of love, an extraordinary kind that lifts you to a different level in life. I have loved many, my husband, my family, my friends, my country, but I was myself in all of them. This was different though. This made me feel different, think differently, and act differently. It was the feeling of motherhood, I guess. All of a sudden it was like there was this tiny thing that would be depending on me totally, who would be needing me there, who had my blood running in her veins and would be calling me Mama and it's wonderful.

★

Aisha was growing quickly. She was smart, funny and her naughtiness was marked on her face. She was deeply in love with Layla, reminding me of myself. She was her Baba's pride and joy and brought happiness into our home. My relationship with Mohammed was closer, deeper, and I prayed that nothing would ever harm it.

My life had changed once Aisha was born. She took most of my time and as she grew older she needed more attention and care. I no longer had time to hang out with my friends in the *bustan*. I would take Aisha once in a while and drop by but they would visit me most of the time. Mohammed and I hardly had any time alone and he was committed to teaching himself English, which made it even harder to communicate. He would come home late from work and, after dinner, burry himself in books as I would put Aisha into bed. By the time he was done we would both be so exhausted that we would go to sleep directly and there were times I couldn't wait for him. I would sleep and would find him still among his books when I woke up for the *fajr* prayers.

I was only thirteen but I was a woman. Everything changed in me; my beliefs, my personality, my character.

"Oh, Khadeeja, you are turning into your mother," Aunty Jameela told me once. "I see my sister, Aisha, in your eyes. She gave you her strength, something I always wished I had."

I believed Aunty Jameela. Mama was always on my mind so much that I was starting to act like her. I was gaining popularity in our *fireej*. I was gaining the people's respect and admiration and everyone valued my opinion. Maybe because I was my mother's daughter, maybe Mohammed's position brought me to this level; after all, to this society all that mattered was your name, where you came from and who you were married to.

"You have her beauty, her intelligence, her wisdom," Mohammed told me. "But there is a side of you that will always be childish, naughty and playful. It's what I love most about you."

Maybe he was right. There were times when after I'd put Aisha to sleep and Mohammed would be in his room with his books when I would sneak into the guest room with Layla and talk to her like I did in the old good times. She remained my best friend, a faithful friend who grew with me every single day. Sometimes I wished I could take her to bed, and sing to her, to sleep, and at other times I would close my eyes and go into a journey to the past, to the old days, Mama's days, and relive years gone by. I was happy with my life but it was always good to go back home, to a world where no one was allowed other than Layla and I.

Chapter Five

Aisha was only two when I got pregnant again but I suffered a miscarriage after I slipped in the bathroom and hurt my back severely.

It was the first time Mohammed and I had a fight. He wanted me to sell my mama's house and I couldn't even allow myself to think about the matter. How could I? It was my home. I was born there. It's where I would go to think or be alone or dream about Mama. I didn't want him to take that away from me. He didn't have the right to take that away from me and he knew that.

"But Khadeeja, you walk all the way to your mother's house to clean all by yourself. Until when are you going to do that?"

He didn't know how much that house meant to me. Mama was there; though I couldn't see her she was there, her soul was there. I felt her holding me, embracing me as I walked in. She was really there.

"Khadeeja, you are pregnant, you can't do that any more. I gave you all the time you wanted to grieve for your mother but it's too much, this is too much, it's got to stop."

And we fought. He was trying to prove his point and I was trying to protect mine. We were getting nowhere. He stormed out of the house and I locked myself in my room and cried.

Aisha was fast asleep. I was still in my room sitting on the floor. My cheeks were still wet from tears but I had stopped crying. I was thinking about Mohammed, worried as a matter of fact. Suddenly I felt warm between my legs. I felt wet and warm. There was pressure in my abdomen. Then there was pain. I tried to stand up but I couldn't. I tried to cry for help but there was no one there, the maid was in her room she wouldn't be able to hear me. I regretted fighting with Mohammed. I wanted him here; if I hadn't fought with him then he would have been here with me.

"Oh my God, stay where you are, I will be right back ma'am. Please don't move, I will come back," shouted the maid. She was checking on baby Aisha when she heard my moaning and found me on the floor.

I was crying when Aunty Jameela ran into the room. I knew something was wrong with me but I didn't know to what extent. My temperature was rising and the warm thing between my thighs was blood. I was two months pregnant and now I was losing my baby, I was going through a miscarriage.

Aunty Jameela and the maid carried me to the bed. They placed towels under me and Aunty Jameela held my hand as she prayed for mercy. Mohammed walked in. His eyes seemed to pop out of his face as he saw the blood on the floor first and then my sweaty face on the bed.

"I am so sorry! It's all my fault," he cried as he ran towards me.

"I knew it, you hit her, you fool, didn't you? You don't fool me mister," screamed Aunty Jameela.

"No, he didn't do anything, we only had an argument."

"There are no more good men on this planet."

"My husband is a good man and I love him very, very much, Aunty Jameela. Would you please leave us alone? He didn't do anything."

"I will go now, but I will never forgive you if you hurt my sister's daughter, you hear me?" she said angrily and barged out of the room.

Mohammed sat next to me. He held my hand close to his heart. His eyes were wide open; those of a concerned person. He was filled with regret and so was I. He tried to hold me, to hug me, but I was in so much pain. He tried to pray but there was so much to say.

"I am so sorry. This is your house as much as it was your mother's. You can do with it whatever you feel like."

"No, it's my fault, I should have never disobeyed you in the first place. You were worried about me but I was inconsiderate."

"You have to rest. Don't think about anything now. We can always talk about it tomorrow."

"I am so sorry. I know you wanted this child."

"We can always have another, Khadeeja, don't think about that. We have Aisha now, and when you are strong enough we can try again."

"You are a very good man, Mohammed."

"And you are the best wife in the whole wide world."

Mohammed sat next to me, played with my hair at times and prayed at other times. I was in pain, like labor pain, but his presence made things feel so much better. The night was long but with the first signs of light it was all over. I could finally sleep. I lost my baby but it was okay, Mohammed said it was okay; it was the start of a new day after all.

Yet that didn't stop us from getting pregnant again. We had a growing family, something Mohammed dreamt of and wanted. Birth control was unheard of in Bahrain in those days and I kept on getting pregnant which for people who could afford to keep a big family like us was a good thing, a blessing, a gift from God.

Fatima and Mariam came next, two beautiful girls, both very different yet very much alike. Though Mohammed was content I wanted a boy. Boys were always closer to their mothers and I wanted someone to carry Mohammed's name. I loved my girls, I didn't mind if I had more, but a boy in the family would also be nice.

It was only two years later that God answered my prayers. I was pregnant again and nine months later I had the most beautiful boy in the world, Nader.

Nader looked so much like his father, yet Auntie Jameela insisted he had my Baba's eyes.

"Oh, you should have called him Abdullah," she would say.

He was handsome and a good baby, very quiet, very calm. I had so many dreams for my Nader but I guess God had other plans.

Nader was five years old, playing with his younger sister, Dana, as I was breast-feeding newly born baby, Abdul-Jabbar, when I heard a scream followed by sudden quietness. I ran out with Abdul-Jabbar still clinging to my breasts to find Nader across the floor with no movement whatsoever. I gave Aisha the baby and ran to Nader to find him unconscious and a scorpion walking across his arms. It was black as death with a tail that stood up like a pole and as I pushed it away with my slippers and crushed it hard, I let out a scream for help that brought the entire neighborhood to the door. The women stayed with the children as the men carried Nader and rushed to the hospital. I sat there shivering, praying and crying, not knowing what to do. I wanted to go to the hospital yet my legs wouldn't carry me and I waited, filled with fear and worries until Mohammed came home. The ladies tried to comfort me but there was no force in the world that would have comforted me at that instance.

"Where is he? Why isn't he with you?" I asked in tears as Mohammed walked in.

"He can't come. Khadeeja, you have to be strong, you have to face this with faith," he managed to say as I feared the worst.

"Is he gone?"

"No, but he will be, any time. There was nothing the doctors could do. The poison was already in his blood. I came to get you so we could be by his side until God decides his fate."

Just as Mohammed was about to help me get up to my feet there was a knock on the door. It was the hospital's ambulance that carried Nader.

"The hospital is packed, we have no extra beds," they said.

"But the doctors said..."

"We're sorry, there is nothing we could do."

Mohammed was angry. After all these years, after all that he had done for that hospital. Was it too much to ask to keep his boy there? Was it too much to respect his feelings? He was also having doubts about the hospital. Did they really try their best? Could they have done anything more to save him?

They brought him in as I cleared my bed for him. He looked pale and blue; I couldn't believe he was my son. I stayed by his bed for two days just watching him, staring at his beautiful face. I couldn't afford losing him; this couldn't be happening but it was. How could a scorpion bite take away my son from me? How did it happen?

By the end of the second day Nader was moaning and had a high fever. I held him in my arms trying to ease his pain, wishing that it had happened to me instead of him. His head fell on my breast and as I watched him struggling to breathe I cried in silence. He looked at me with innocence and forced a smile on his face.

"Mama, don't be sad," he said.

"Hush baby, you need to rest."

"I had a dream, Mama. I had a beautiful white horse and he carried me far away, but I was happy, I was not afraid."

"May you always be happy my baby."

"I love you, Mama."

"I love you too."

I cried; I could not help but cry. I was not prepared for his death. I was not prepared to let go, not yet. He asked me to describe heaven and I tried to memorize every detail on his innocent face; his round face, his shiny eyes, his cheek bones, his pink lips. He was a handsome boy, a weak handsome boy. He moaned and I prayed for his pain to go away.

"What's heaven like, Mama?"

"It's a beautiful place, baby. You can find everything beautiful there, all that your heart desires."

"Would I be able to have cars and motorcycles?"

"Oh yes, and much more," I laughed at his innocence.

"Who will take care of me, Mama? Who will I live with?"

"Allah will be with you. No one will ever take care of you as He will. And you know what, my mama is there too."

"Your Mama?"

"Yes. She is a wonderful lady. She is beautiful and funny and you will love her, I know you will."

"Don't cry then; see, you know I will be alright."

"I love you, Nader, I love you so much."

"Don't cry, Mama, I want to go to heaven."

But I couldn't not cry. I held him for the last time and cried. I prayed and cried. I recited the Quran and cried. I cried like I never did before. I was saying goodbye to my son, to my little child, to my angel.

In a moment's notice my son left me, he was gone, leaving behind an innocent smile on his face, a smile I carved in my heart forever, never to be forgotten. I cried, I held him in my arms and cried aloud. The children came running in and Mohammed fell to his knees covering his face with his hands. The children cried too. They each took turns kissing their brother goodbye and it only broke my heart even more.

★

The neighborhood men came to help Mohammed with the funeral arrangements. Nader was still on my bed, all in white, the angel he always was. Mohammed called me in to bid him farewell before they took him and I couldn't let go. He felt so cold yet at peace. He reminded me of Mama as he lay there motionless in white. Was it just yesterday when he was brought to me for the first time covered with white on the day he was born? Was it yesterday my baby called me Mama for the first time and took his first step on this stone floor towards me? I could still hear him laugh and play with his brothers and sisters. I could still see him climb the palm tree and race his friends to the *dukkan*. Did I really lose him forever?

Nader was gone; he left me forever, never to return.

I saw the men carry him across the *housh*. He was placed towards the *ka'aba* as they all prayed behind him in unity. Nader was then carried to the graveyard to be buried next to his grandmother, which was a comfort to me, knowing that she would take really good care of him, even better than I would have myself.

Yes it was a miserable time, but I wouldn't have made it without Mohammed. Again he was the support though he needed support himself. I struggled to get my life back together, though I hated everything about it, yet I had to force myself to stand up on my feet for my children, for my baby who still needed his mother's milk and for the innocent faces who missed their brother and their happy home. God gave me patience and only through that patience and a husband like Mohammed I was me again, though the pain haunted me for the rest of my life.

I blamed Layla for not taking care of my son. I blamed myself. But I knew we couldn't do much for it was God's will and I had to accept it. Layla found consolation with my children, trying to give me strength from time to time but I needed time alone, away from it all. I needed to put myself together and this time I had to do it on my own.

Mohammed tried to run away from his feelings. He was sad but didn't want to show it. He didn't cry, didn't allow himself to cry, even when he was alone. He would think, he would remember, he would dry my tears but he wouldn't allow himself to cry.

"You know why this happened? You know why you lost a son?" said Saleh, a family friend who had just arrived from Farris, Iran.

"It's God's will, Saleh, I can't deny that," said Mohammed.

"Of course it is but there is a reason behind it, everything happens for a reason. If you don't take this warning seriously you will lose the whole family, your family."

"What do you mean?"

"Your father is angry at you, Mohammed. You left Persia against his will and you disobeyed him. This is a curse and it will haunt you as long as your father remains angry. You have to leave; you have to go see him. He is an old man and if he dies angry I assure you, you will never be happy."

Mohammed was troubled with these words. As an educated man, there was a part of him that didn't believe such rubbish, but there was another part that was frightened and hurt from losing a child, he could not risk losing another. He loved his family and was willing to do anything for them. He spent long sleepless nights trying to decide, wanting to do the right thing. I was pregnant four months after Nader died but suffered another miscarriage a month into my pregnancy and with that happening Mohammed insisted on seeing his father. I knew it was one of the most difficult decisions he had to make in his life but he was concerned. He was haunted with the curse and ached for happiness and security to return to his sad home.

"Khadeeja, we are going to Farris," he told me one evening.

"But the children?"

"We'll take them, we'll take them all. I will help you, don't worry."

I was unable to change his mind and we took the first boat to Farris. The children were happy but he was worried. He could not face his father after all that time and now he was left with no choice but to give in and return to his homeland. I didn't know how to feel. I was scared and I was happy. I was scared because I didn't know what was going to happen between Mohammed and his father, and I was happy because I had always wanted to see

Farris. The sea was rough and some people were seasick, but the children managed to fill their time with games and stories. Mohammed was lost in deep thought and I prayed for Allah's support; my family has been through enough already. I wished I was able to do something to ease my husband's pain but there was nothing I could do but give him the space he needed to think. It was between him and his father and he had to face him alone.

★

"Khadeeja, wake up, we're are there already," I heard Mohammed say.

The sun rays hurt my eyes, I could hardly open them. I heard the sea gulls as they surrounded the boat and people screaming in Persian from every corner. The children were clapping and jumping for joy, waiting for their adventure to start as Mohammed carried our bags. We walked to the closest carriage; I realized how different Farris was from Bahrain. Mohammed sat next to the carriage driver while we took our places behind them. The roads were made of stone bricks, the whitewashed houses were like mosques, and trees were everywhere. Everything was different, the way they dressed, they way they lived; even their language was a bit different than the Persian I knew.

The carriage stopped in front of a mansion. The rusty gates squeaked as they moved back and forth loosely, and as we took our first steps on the stone pathway it started to rain. Was it a good or bad sign? I yearned to know. A woman came running with open arms screaming, crying, and laughing all at the same time. Poor Yuma Amina just couldn't believe that her son had finally come home.

We were taken into the house as servants took our belongings into the guest rooms. Mohammed's sisters were all over the children while Yuma Amina went to prepare the food. There was laughter everywhere, laughter that echoed through empty hallways and lonely walls. It was a dull house. The long velvet drapes blocked the sunlight and the naked rooms screamed with boredom. I walked around the house, drowsy from a long journey but filled with curiosity of what was hidden within it, what secrets these walls bore, and how did such a house raise a prefect man like Mohammed.

Mohammed though walked slowly to the west end of the house. He looked nervous and I could see his shivering hands as he tried to open the grand doors in front of him. I wanted to hold him, I wanted to run and embrace him, to tell him that everything was going to be just fine but I couldn't do that. I didn't know if it was going to be alright. I didn't know if Mohammed's worried heart was going to be peaceful again. I watched him and whispered him a prayer.

The children were playing in the guest quarters; it was more like a garden filled with flowers and plants of all kinds. The windows were surrounded with colorful mosaic tiles and the doors were painted in red. The whitewashed walls gave a beautiful reflection on the small water pool and the carved stone flowers on the sides of the main entrance looked so much alive.

I wondered why the guest quarters was so much more beautiful than the main house and I was relieved we were going to stay in a livelier place for I couldn't bear that dullness.

Yuma Amina didn't want Mohammed to meet his father alone after all that time. Like Mohammed, she too was concerned; the happy face she had when we first arrived was nowhere to be seen. She took me by the hand and ran behind Mohammed who was still standing in front of that brown wooden door, the big door, and I wondered what was behind that door that brought so much fear to my husband and his mother.

"I think you can ease the tension up if you came in with us, dear," she said as we approached that grand door.

I was surprised to find Mohammed still standing in front of that door. Was he too afraid? Was he ever going to walk in? Did he need to be pushed in as Mama had pushed me into my new house on my wedding day? He looked at us, trying to hide his concern, and turned the metal knob on the door.

Mohammed walked in and we followed him very quietly. I wasn't prepared at all for such a thing. I prayed for peace as I held Yuma Amina's hand tightly. I wished it was Mama's hand. I wished she was there with me to protect me. I have always believed that Mohammed was my protector after Mama died but today he needed protection himself and I needed Mama. The room was dark. The walls were covered with shelves of neverending books and the burning incense filled the air.

"Hello, Father," said Mohammed, very softly.

The father was sitting on his *sujadh* in the corner of the room, opposite a large painted window. He looked old, too old to move on his own. The holy Quran was sitting on a stand in front of him. Though he was not the town's sheikh any more he managed to keep his status among the people for his knowledge in Islam. The people still went to him for religious matters and to have his blessings. He continued to read the Quran and we stood there in silence. I could see tears in the corner of Mohammed's eyes and Yuma Amina was trembling. His voice was strong and clear and his heavy body moved slightly as he read the versus. Once he completed the section he closed the holy book gently lifted his wrinkled hands to the sky and whispered a prayer. He looked up at Mohammed, took off his glasses and placed them carefully on a short stool next to him.

"Come here my son," he said.

I watched as Mohammed walked towards his father wondering if my father would have looked that way had he been alive.

"Amina, who is in the room with you?" he asked.

"Sheikh this is Khadeeja, your daughter-in-law."

"Come here child; come let me see you,"

I was too scared to look at him as I approached them. He made me sit next to him where he could have a good look at me.

"So you are the only daughter of Sheikh Abdullah are you?"

"Yes, Sheikh, I am."

I didn't want to be the center of attention. I wanted them to be alone, Mohammed and his father. There was so much Mohammed wanted to say, so much to be said.

"Mohammed," he finally said, "did you forget that I am alive?"

"Father, I didn't mean to leave that way. I didn't want to disobey you but I wanted more than what you wanted for me."

"You should have told me your plans."

"I couldn't, there was little time. You had already arranged for my departure to the Islamic school."

"But you never came back after all this time?"

"I knew you were angry, I was too ashamed to see you again."
"And why now?"
"Because of my family, father. We need your forgiveness, we need your blessing." Mohammed was trying to pull himself together as he told his father about Nader, about my miscarriages. He told him about the curse and why we need his blessings so badly.

"You should know better than that son. You should know that such a curse does not exist. What happened was God's will. He is testing you, your faith, and your patience. You have to ask for His forgiveness, not mine."

"Father, I have accomplished so much. I am happy now, I am happy with my life."

"And I am happy for you, Mohammed." And he smiled. It was the first time I saw him smile. His thick brows curled up under his wrinkled forehead. He looked at his son with so much affection and love. He opened his arms and Mohammed threw himself into his arms and laughed as we all did.

"Thank you father, thank you so much, I never thought you'd ever forgive me."

"If the good Lord forgives, how dare I not forgive? You are my son and you mean the world to me. As long as you are a good man and a good believer you have my love, blessing and my prayer."

We spent a wonderful time in Farris until the unexpected happened. Mohammed found his father dead in his room when he went to call him for lunch only ten days after we had arrived. He had died on his *sujadhh* while he was praying. Mohammed was devastated and sat in his father's room for long hours, away from people, away from us. Two weeks later he had to force himself to return to Bahrain. Though I tried to convince him to stay with his mother, he had to return to his own work. Staying in Farris would do him no good, he believed.

I was happy Mohammed saw his father before he died. I was happy he had spent the last days of his life with him. I was happy that my children had a chance to see their grandfather, that great scholar who all Muslims were proud of. He was a great man, a wise man, and a loving father. He had a pure heart and a soul of gold. We loved him, we all did, and his death was a great loss to us all.

Chapter Six

I had six daughters and two sons, starting with Aisha then Fatima, Mariam, Dana, Abdul-Jabbar, Lulwa, Abdurrahman and Noor, and I was two months pregnant with my ninth child. I had already lost three children, Nader and two miscarriages, and I was hoping this one would survive.

My life was a rollercoaster yet it was good. Mohammed worked harder now and sometimes we'd also have patients come to the house and he would take a look at them to see if they needed a specialist or if some homemade remedies would do. It was an open house really and that was not a bad thing; we both loved people and I was raised in an open house so I was used to it in a way.

But as time passed he was starting to change, my Mohammed. His humor seemed to have disappeared and his face was that of a tired old man. He was either buried in his books or with patients and I was missing him. There was something he didn't want to say and it seemed like keeping himself busy was his only answer.

"I have to sell the house." He surprised me one day.

"Why, are we in need of money? Has something happened?" I said fearfully.

"No, but I have found a better job and we need to move somewhere closer."

"Were you looking for a job? Are you uncomfortable with this one? Why didn't you tell me?"

"No, no, I just got a better offer."

"Mohammed, are you hiding something? You have been killing yourself with work lately, you look tired, we hardly sit and talk, I don't understand what's happening."

"Khadeeja, I want you and the kids to be happy. I am fine, it's just that I found a better deal and I want to be able to spend more time with you and the kids, and this new job is a good pay and gives me more time."

In a way my mind believed him but my heart didn't. There was something he didn't want me to know and I couldn't make him say it. And the days passed. We sold the house, our first house, the one I had all my children in, and moved to a rented house. What a difference. We no longer had the *bustan* view; we no longer had a nearby well and an easy access to the sea. The *housh* was nearly half our old one and we didn't have as many windows as we used to, which made it a bit gloomy. We only had two bedrooms, one living room, one kitchen, one bathroom and the guest area consisted of one room and a bathroom.

I didn't understand why Mohammed would bring us such a house after we were in an owned, comfortable home. It did not make sense. It was a big transition and I knew it, it was a transition from richness to poorness and I was worried.

"It's just a temporary place, Khadeeja, really there is nothing to worry about," he would insist.

The days went by and nothing happened. The kids were all in one room. We couldn't even use the guest room because Mohammed's patients and guests were coming and going all the time. I couldn't mention how uncomfortable we were; he would lose his temper easily and his dignity wouldn't let me sell Mama's house now or even live there until he found a better place.

"Mohammed, why won't you talk to me?"

"There's nothing to say."

"With all that is going on you want me to believe that there is nothing you have to say?"

"You worry for no reason."

"I wish you were right, I wish I could believe you."

"Khadeeja, you are a good woman, you are pure and kind. There are things in life you might not be able to understand."

"I am not a child!"

"You are not a child but you are innocent. Please don't ask me too many questions. I promise you everything will be just fine. We will all be fine."

"You say this as if I am a stranger, as if I don't see the pain in your eyes and the mystification in your heart."

"Come here, sleep in my arms like you used to when we first got married. Throw everything behind your back and sleep in peace, my love. Tomorrow is another day."

★

It was late at night, Mohammed still had guests and the kids were asleep. I had finished my house chores and was aching to sleep but wanted to wait for Mohammed. I couldn't help holding Layla, combing her hair, and whispering a lullaby. Layla was always my savior whenever I wanted to run away from reality for she sucked me into her world. She was still as beautiful as when I got her, still my best friend. I was 23 but Layla and I were still one soul in two bodies.

"Still awake?" Mohammed surprised me.

"Still awake. Are you done?" I said as I hid my Layla under the bed.

"Finally. How are the children?"

"Fine. Would you like to eat something?"

"No I want to sleep, I am very tired. Khadeeja, come sit next to me for a little bit."

I walked towards him and he seemed so sad I thought I saw a tear. He said nothing, just sat there staring at me, looking into my eyes as if trying to read my thoughts. He was shivering and his face said so many things yet the words were lost in a deep contemplation.

Finally and after a long period of silence he managed to spell out some words while trying to hold back the tears. "Will you ever hate me?"

What an absurd question, but what was it that made him ask such a question? What is it that he was hiding, why did he fear my hatred? There were too many unanswered questions and I didn't know how to react, what exactly should I say?

"Mohammed, how can you ask me such a question? After all these years, after all we've been through together, you should know the answer."

"I want to hear it from you. I want your lips to speak these words I need to know sweet Khadeeja."

"You are my husband; you are the man I lived with for the past eleven years through good and bad. I can't imagine a day without you. You are all I have left Mohammed. How can I ever hate you? How can I? You have always respected me, always treated me with kindness and love and always understood me. I love you so much that I would give up my life for you."

And he cried. I had never seen Mohammed cry before and I was frightened that something really bad had happened. But he didn't answer my questions, he just kissed my hand and forehead, held me tight and cried himself to sleep.

I stayed awake all night thinking, praying, trying to understand what was going on. At times my mind told me stuff that my heart didn't believe and at other times my heart told me things my mind just couldn't accept, but something I was sure of, Mohammed was running away from something and what ever that thing was it was going to affect our relationship.

I heard the call to the *fajr* prayers and watched Mohammed as he walked to a close-by mosque. He usually prayed at home but somehow decided to go to the mosque that day. When he returned he held my hand as we walked towards the children's room. He stood there watched them breathe heavily as a tear ran down his cheekbone. He kissed them one by one, blew a kiss for Nader and headed towards the door.

"I am going to work."

"Mohammed, why don't you rest today? I can't let you go to work today, not like this. Look at you, Mohammed, please stay."

"No, no, I have to leave. I know someday you will understand and forgive me."

And he rushed out the door. I didn't understand what he meant at the time, "someday you will understand and forgive me," what was he trying to tell me? I felt like running after him but something stopped me as I heard my heart whisper in pain, "You won't see him again, Khadeeja, Mohammed left you."

I was right. Mohammed did leave me. He never came home after that day and I was left back with eight children and expecting my ninth in a few months. There was nothing I could do, I was sad, I was angry, I was confused. I needed to know why he left me but there was no one there that could help me. I was all alone, in pain, depressed and lonely. The house that was filled with people once upon a time was empty with hardly a knock on the door. People turned their faces like they never knew me and the neighbors saw me as a disgrace to the *fireej*.

I knew he was gone but I tried to convince myself otherwise. Maybe he had to go on a trip. Maybe something came up. He wouldn't leave me. He loved me, I knew he did, but nights passed and I gave up. He wasn't coming home. He won't come into my arms, he deserted my arms. Did he not love me? Was it all a lie then? Was he a lie?

I could never be able to describe how I felt at the time. I would sleep with Layla in my arms, aching for comfort, and sometimes Aisha, who was eleven at the time, would wake me up from a nightmare as I would scream for Mama.

Mama. What would she do if she had to go through this? It was true that Baba left her too, but he died, he didn't walk out; and being a widow was something accepted in the society, even respected, but a woman whose husband had left her was something else. She was a strong woman, would she have cared? Would she leave and go to another neighborhood? I didn't know but there was something I did know. Mama loved me so much that she would forget about herself and think of me, my future, my happiness and my well-being. She would face the whole world for me and so I decided that it was what I would do. I had to force myself out of this depression and sadness. Mohammed had left me already and there was nothing I could do to make him come back. I had my children and they were everything I had left; how could I possibly neglect them because their father hurt me. It isn't their fault; they should not and will not pay for it.

"Mama, where is Baba?" Noor asked me as we were having a light supper one evening.

"Your father had to travel. He was sent to a different place for sometime to do some work," I answered desolately.

"I miss Baba, when will he return, Mama?" said Lulwa.

"I don't know, baby, I don't know. When he is done with his work he will come back."

"Yeah, it was always work he was in love with anyway, why should he care about us?" said Abdurrahman bitterly.

"Don't you dare say that about Baba, Abdurrahman. Have you ever even considered why Baba is so tired with work? To send you and your sisters to school. To give you a good life, a respectful life, and to secure your future. Abdurrahman, no father loves his children the way your father loves you. Don't you forget that no matter what happens, you understand?

"Yes, Mama," he said regretfully.

It was difficult. The children asked so many questions I myself needed answers for and I didn't know what to say. I didn't want them to build any hostility towards their father but his sudden disappearance had affected them negatively. Was there any hope of his return; I didn't know. I should tell them the truth but I needed someone to tell me the truth myself.

"I can't believe Mohammed would do such a thing," cried Aunty Jameela. "But why? He seemed to be very happy with you, Khadeeja, was there something wrong?"

"I don't know, Aunty Jameela. We were happy but something was wrong and he just wouldn't tell me."

"Do you think there's another woman?"

"I don't know, but he was always busy. Too busy to even have a drink of water, to be looking at another woman or even be with another woman. He was always at home in the guest room either studying or with people. How could he be with another woman."

Aunty Jameela was filling my head with all these suspicions that I didn't want to think of or even consider. It was too painful; the thought of my Mohammed with another woman.

"My child, don't blame yourself. He must need some time off, like a break from all the pressure maybe, and in no time he will be back. Don't give up, God always has a good plan for people, you just keep faith in Him and you'll surely see his mercy."

"Amen, Aunty Jameela, amen."

I did have a slight hope for his return. Something inside me told me he would return, I just didn't know when. I wished Aunty Jameela was right. Maybe he needed some time alone, but why leave in such a way? Why desert me with nothing said or explained?

"Only time could tell," I guessed.

★

I am a coward, said Mohammed to himself, I have walked out on my wife, the love of my life, my children, my pride and joy.

He took the first ship to Dubai, the land of dreams and promises, but to him it was escaping from the harsh reality to the unknown. Never did he expect his life to turn that way. Never did he think that he would lose all his privileges the moment he lost his job; his life was at stake, his dignity was stabbed. He had to leave.

They will never forgive me I know; they will hate me for it. But they are better off without me. It will be difficult at first but things will be better. I know they will. I know. He tried to convince himself.

He could already see the twinkling lights from a distance and he knew there was no return. He had left a whole life behind and was about to walk on a land that would bring him a new life, a different life. He wasn't happy but he wasn't sad. His heart was at home, with his wife and children, but his mind took him to a better future, for him and his family.

The sea was calm and the sky was black. There was nothing out there but the glittering lights of a not-so-far-away land and the whisper of a cold breeze. What was waiting for him he didn't know. Where would he go and how would he start? He had nothing with him but twenty Dirham; he left it all in Khadeeja's box hoping she would find it. Twenty Dirham might take him to a three star hotel and buy him some food for a week but what if he couldn't find a job before that, where would he go next? He knew his in-laws were there, but how on earth was he thinking of them after what he did to their sister? They would kill him. He wished he was asleep in Khadeeja's arms. He wished he could kiss the children one more time but it was too late now. He only prayed that one day God would forgive him so his family would forgive him too.

"Where would you like to go, sir?" he heard someone scream at him. He was lost in this deep well of thoughts, his own thoughts, that he did not realize they had arrived already. It was hot, the cool breeze had disappeared somewhere in the sea, it was after midnight but the port was as busy as it would have been during the day. There was the porter with the luggage running left and right. There were tears of goodbyes and welcomes, there was screams of sailors and captains mixed with the foul smell of fish, spoiled food and forgotten garbage everywhere. There was so much life yet the sky's darkness seemed to sink into Mohammed, filling him with fear and regret. It was going to be difficult but he had to face it now.

"To the closest hotel please," he answered.

He followed the man to a carriage and suddenly realized he couldn't afford such luxuries any more.

"No, it's alright, if you could just show me the way I would prefer to walk. As you see I have no luggage with me so that won't be a problem."

"As you wish. You walk to the end of this road. Take a left and then the first right and you will find a hotel."

Luckily it wasn't an expensive hotel but a rather cheap one. The location was dull, isolated in a way. The entrance was decorated with cheap golden frames and a neon sign with an arrow pointing to the hotel. The reception was smoky and the smell of alcohol filled the room. It was dark with a faint of red light from hidden windows. It didn't take him long to figure out that it was a dirty hotel, the kind of hotel drunk men would come to for prostitutes. His life was going from bad to worst, he knew that but he had to face it now. He was so tired, frustrated, and sad that he took the first room available and sunk into a deep sleep in no time.

It was just before noon when he was forced to wake up by a banging on the next room wall. At first he could not recall a thing, where he was and why Khadeeja hadn't woken him yet. It was only when he heard the loud voices of drunk men outside that reality struck. He took a quick shower, put his clothes on and ran to seize the day, to look for a job and meet the new world, a world where only he existed, no worries or responsibilities.

Chapter Seven

"Ma'am, you haven't paid the rent for three months now. We also have bills that we want to pay and we need our money." The landlord surprised me early one day.

Three months? Mohammed left without even paying the rent? What was this man thinking? Could this really be happening? Could he really be a coward?

"Don't worry, *haji* Abdullah, I will have the money for you. Please forgive me but I am going through difficult times."

"Ma'am, why don't you go stay with your brother in Dubai? You can't live alone with these children, who will protect you?"

"God will, *haji* Abdullah, God is watching over me and my children until Mohammed returns."

"He won't be coming back, Khadeeja, it's about time you believed us."

"I believe that only Allah knows what will happen to me and whatever that will be I will welcome it in contentment."

"God bless you and forgive me. If it was up to me I would not accept one *fils* (coin) but I have a family to feed and I have my sick parents and…"

"*Haji* Abdullah, I don't want your pity. I just needed some time to think and plan."

"I understand."

What a situation. What should I do? I had nothing left. I sold all my jewelry to pay for necessities and everyday provisions. Food was scarce and school payments were expensive. The rent was overdue and there was no one to turn to. All those who were once my friends disappeared and for the first time in my life I needed my brothers.

★

There I was. A mother. More like a single mother. In an isolated place. Aching. In pain. An indescribable pain. I didn't know if anything was fair any more. Lonely was too little a word to describe what I was going through. Regret was too harsh a word for I had beautiful little angels that wouldn't be here if all this hadn't happened. Frightened? Yes I was. Scared and worried about the future, mine and theirs.

It all happened in a flash of light. A nightmare, an unforgettable nightmare. I knew I was being punished but for something I hadn't done. How dare he? After all I had done for him, all the things I gave up. How could he deceive the trust of my whole family, forget all that he promised? And why? Why do I still love him? Why didn't I walk out before he did? Why didn't I see what was coming when the signs were there the whole time. Why was my innocence taken from me so soon?

> Though you hurt me so much I still miss you,
> Though you threw my love away, I still want you,
> Though you only brought pain, I still cherish you
> But if you ever come back, I will not take you

I sang. I sang myself to sleep and I sang myself out of bed. I sang to forget, for hope, for peace. Yet reality was harsh, so harsh that I could feel my heart break more and more by the hour.

Was it me or was it what men do? Baba died and left Mama. Aziz and Hassan left Mama. But Mama had me. I was there till she died and left me, as Baba left me, as Aziz and Hassan left me, as Nader left me, as Mohammed left me. I was the one left behind, all alone with little angels who knew nothing about life.

> What is left of me is a book of memories,
> To read alone the rest of my life,
> Waiting for the day till I met death
> Only then no longer will I strife

Yes, memories were the worst. Promises. Lies. Where was love? If there was any. What was it about then? All this time. Deceit?

Dishonesty? Could it be? Was I that stupid? That blind to believe him all this time?

Too many things. I could not handle it. Layla, where were you? Why didn't you tell me? You must have seen it coming? Why didn't you warn me? You were there every day. Every single day, watching over me but you didn't say a word. You stared with your still eyes, you must have seen it coming. Layla?

I wished she would talk just this one time so I would know I was not alone. Only once. But reality was way too harsh. I was only a child, still a child with all these little lives behind me. God have mercy on me.

*

Writing a letter to Hassan was one of the most difficult things I had to do. I was never close to my brothers. The age difference was huge and by the time I was old enough to understand and know all those around me, Aziz and Hassan were married and off in a far away place. I didn't get along with their wives, who were both drowning in the world of materialism. They never welcomed me or Mama and didn't bother to show up for Mama's funeral. How could I ask him to come? What should I say? It took me a whole week until I was able to and was courageous enough to sit down with Aisha and write the letter:

Hassan,
Mohammed is out of town and I can't take care of the children alone. Can you please keep me company for a couple of weeks?"
Truly yours,
Khadeeja

I didn't want to tell him Mohammed had left me. I didn't want him to make plans to take me to Dubai with him but I had to call for him for he was always nicer to me than Aziz. I knew he was going to get shocked, finding us in such a house after living in a big house. I knew I would have to prepare myself for his anger and desire in revenge for what has happened to me, and I was prepared for the worst.

And the day came. Well, it was a difficult moment but no time to be emotional as I welcomed Hassan as he arrived with a bagful of bad news.

"My dear sister, I had no idea you knew nothing about your husband," he calmly said.

"Hassan, I don't know where he went or if he's safe. I don't know when he'll be back but there is so much out here and I don't know what to do until his return."

"I wished so bad that it wouldn't be me who'd give you such news but I'm afraid I have no choice."

"Is Mohammed hurt? Is he dead? Tell me please, this is too much to handle."

"No, no, he is alive and fine, but I fear he will not return."

"What? Why? What happened?"

"Mohammed is in Dubai. He married another woman and he's found another job there."

And I felt someone had just slapped me so hard that I lost consciousness. I couldn't believe a word he said. My husband, the father of my children had left me, never to return, and is now with another woman after all that was between us, after all we went through together, leaves me this way all alone, with no one to help, eight hungry children and the ninth about to see the world. How was I going to live? How was I going to survive?

"Oh God, Hassan, what should I do now? Why did he do this Hassan? Why didn't you tell me before?"

"My dear sister, I thought you knew, I thought he had settled things here before he left. I had no idea you were left behind with nothing, not even the simple truth. Mohammed was fired some time ago now and was looking for a job, and as you know, even the rich are now out of jobs. He couldn't face you or the children any more. He couldn't keep up with all the responsibility and was already drowning in loans. He took the easy way out, the selfish one I guess, and ran away to Dubai, met a rich woman, got married, and bought himself a new life, with her money of course."

Hassan had found out about his brother-in-law by coincidence. He was in a *qahwa* in a popular Dubai district where he saw Mohammed in a fancy car with two men, passing by. His curiosity made him ask around for Mohammed's whereabouts and he heard that he was a rich husband now. He moved to Dubai from Bahrain, married a rich man's daughter and inherited everything after the old man died. Hassan knew that Mohammed had left his sister, but what he didn't know was why. After searching for answers through friends, Hassan learned about Mohammed's misfortune with his job and his running away to find a better life in a selfish, irresponsible manner and decided to go to Bahrain to his heartbroken sister. A few days later he received a letter from his sister and in no time packed up and left.

"My Mohammed? No, that isn't like him. My Mohammed has pride, dignity, he has self-respect and vanity, and he wouldn't do such a thing. He would never put himself in such a low position for money. No, Hassan, you are wrong my husband is a good man, he fears God, he will not desert me and the kids for money. He will be back, and when he does our life will catch up from where it stopped. I called you here to help me for the time being, not to wrong my husband and in his house! Now I am even sorry I asked you to come in the first place."

"You don't deserve this, you don't deserve to be left this way and he definitely doesn't deserve your love and respect. It is the truth and it hurts I know, but that doesn't change anything. You lost your husband and it's not your fault life was cruel on you, but you still have your children and you are all they've got. You have to pull yourself together and think wisely with your mind not your heart. It is late now, go get some rest and give some thought to what is it that you want to do. We will talk tomorrow and figure out how things should work."

But I couldn't sleep. I couldn't believe my husband, it was too painful. I couldn't stop myself from crying even though I didn't want to. A part of me said there was so much to cry for yet a part said he was not worth a teardrop. I didn't know what to think. I only grieved with a broken heart and an empty soul. For the first time in my life I was totally in charge of my life and family and I had no idea what to do. I turned to God as I always have done but this time I didn't need to complain, He already knew what had happened to me. This time I only prayed for help, to know the right thing to do, not only for me but for my children as well. I needed guidance and only He was able to protect me from losing my home, my family and my pride.

I was in deep meditation and prayer with tearful eyes and weak body when I heard the first bird sing, marking the start of a new day. I opened my eyes to find the most beautiful scene ahead; a clear sky with the first strikes of light; the whisper of wind as it swayed the palm trees; the tiny drops of dew like stars on the grass; the enchantment of the call to prayer echoing from nearby mosques; and the quiet foot steps of men as they walked to pray. It was a sign, I believed, a sign from the Almighty Lord to lift my spirit and help me up on my feet. It was like He was telling me that there is always a new day with a new life and a new beginning. I had to go on with my life. I will not walk away from my children or leave them to suffer, I will work no matter what it takes, I will keep my family's name and will not accept charity or sympathy from anyone, and I have God on my side to lead me through this. I will challenge Mohammed and this time I will win.

It was not easy; I had to be strong. I had to go against my heart and forget my feelings, I had to. I had cried enough.

★

"Hassan, I want to work. You have to go back to your wife, I only needed someone with me for some time but now I am fine. I think I have a good plan. I have three weeks till the rent deadline and I know I will be fine. Thank you for everything," I told Hassan two days after his arrival.

"Khadeeja, you are my sister. I know we never had the chance to sit and talk, we didn't grow up with each other, it's like we hardly even know each other but that doesn't mean that I will leave you in such a time. Such a thing would anger Mama and we are blood; we have no one but each other."

"But your wife?"

"My wife won't even notice that I'm not around. Besides I told her that I would be here for some time."

And we sat down to talk about our lives. I decided to work as a tailor, something Mama taught me, something I was good at.

Aisha would help me after school and Hassan would open a small *dukkan*, minimarket, and start it off until Abdul-Jabbar and Abdurrahman were old enough to take care of it.

Being a tailor was rather a good start. With the help of Hassan's *dukkan* I was able to pay for five months' rent as well as new clothes for *eid*, our holy ceremony. We could hear laughter again in our home and Hassan and I were forming a wonderful relationship, a relationship that was never there before.

"Hassan, why weren't we close before? You were never around Mama and I were always alone?"

"Life was not always easy, Khadeeja. We couldn't live off Baba's money. We had to go and explore the world. We had to look for a good job, an adventure; we had the chance and we couldn't lose it."

"And did you find what you were looking for?"

"Maybe. I had money, lots of it. My wife was happy, I had a big house, my own car, but I wasn't happy. I wanted Bahrain, my home, my childhood land. I missed it; I missed the people, the palm trees, even the hot weather and humidity."

"Why didn't you come back?"

"She didn't want to come back."

"Your wife?"

"Yes. She took control of my business, my money, my home, and I am with nothing, just a person who still lives there."

"Why didn't you tell us before? Mama would have welcomed you with open arms."

"I didn't want to hurt her. She had gone through enough already."

Hassan, the kind-hearted, quiet person, had trusted his wife with his own life. He gave her all she wanted with no hesitation but Haifa was not trustworthy. She was in it for the money, Hassan's money, and when she took it all she had an affair with Hassan's best friend. He knew about it, he knew about it the whole time but didn't care, or he grew not to care. He loved her, she was his wife but there was nothing left of him to fight this. He was already too tired, he was growing old.

"What about Aziz was he there for you?"

"Aziz was too busy with his own life. He has no time for me and my problems. Khadeeja, I have been thinking of selling Mama's home. Aziz wants his share and it's too big for us to live in – we can't afford it."

"Sell Mama's house? That's all we have left with good memories."

"But the expenses are too much and school fees are coming up, not to forget Aisha is at the age of marriage and in no time we will have to prepare her. Abdul-Jabbar and Abdurrahman will be going to high school and we should start planning for higher education like college and stuff."

Wow. My brother was thinking about my own children more than I was, like they were his own. I couldn't help but cry. I never imagined him to be so understanding of my situation. I thought he'd force me to go back with him to Dubai, but he respected my feelings. I thought he'd blame me for Mohammed's desertion but he tried to create a new life, make me forget the past and concentrate on my children. Hassan was a good man. He didn't deserve a wife who took him for his money and threw him with nothing. He was so passionate, loving and devoted to the children, and the kids were so happy around him. They would run to welcome him when he'd come home after *maghreb* and he would tell them a story after dinner and tuck them into bed. I thanked God for writing that letter and I thanked God for sending me Hassan in such a terrible time.

*

We sold the house, Mama's house. Hassan sent Aziz's share to Dubai and gave me his share.

"Keep this with you. You never know when you might need it," he told me.

"No, Hassan, my share is enough."

"It was difficult enough for you to see Mama's house sold; and we are living together, if I needed it I won't hesitate to ask for it."

"May God bless you, dear brother, may God bless you."

There was something uncomfortable about Hassan. He reminded me of the time Mohammed was hiding losing his job. Was there something wrong with the *dukkan*? Was he going to leave soon? Even if he did it was his right; he had a life of his own besides worrying about me and my children. His wife was waiting for him, maybe they could work things out and I already felt guilty for having him leave her all this time.

"Hassan, you are tired, why don't you go to Dubai? Haifa your wife must be waiting for you."

"What makes you say that, you want to get rid of me already? I just came here?" he said jokingly.

"No, but I see you sad and it's like you miss your wife and your old life and I messed up your life."

"No, it's not like that, I just received a letter from Dubai, one that carried bad news."

"What news? Why didn't you tell me? Is Haifa alright?"

"I'm afraid not. Haifa died."

He broke down like a small child and I didn't know what to do. How could he hide such a thing? I felt guilty. He should have been where he belonged with his wife but I had to drag him up here with all selfishness. I knew she was a bad person, she had committed adultery and she should have been stoned to death, but I had a feeling that it could have worked out only if Hassan had returned. God was gracious and forgiving after all.

"Hassan, why didn't you tell me?"

"You have enough to think of and I couldn't talk about it, I wasn't ready at all."

"Was she sick?"

"She was perfectly healthy but the letter said that she fell into the well as she was fetching some water. The bucket got stuck and as she was trying to pull it up she lost balance and fell. It seemed no one knew about her until they saw the body."

"I am very sorry Hassan, I am sorry that you weren't there for her."

"It's God's will and I am content with whatever God has set for me."

"Why don't you stay home for some days and I'll send Abdul-Jabbar to take your place in the *dukkan*."

"Leave the boy with his studies, I am fine, Khadeeja, really, there is no need for feeling guilty. I want to keep myself busy that way I won't have time to feel alone. Well, let's look on the bright side, she wasn't good to me anyway." He let out a rather sad laugh.

"Let's remember the dead with their goodness." I tried to calm him down.

"Well then, I might as well forget her," he said as he walked out.

Chapter Eight

"Mama why don't you rest? Fatima and I will take care of the housework. You look tired, and you heard what Aunty Jameela said about bending too much in your eighth month," said Aisha in a worried tone.

I got up from the kitchen stool and looked at my little daughter who wasn't little any more. When did she grow up to be such a beautiful girl? She looked like my mama in a way. She has always been there around me, taking care of me and her little brothers and sisters. She was there aching for her father, hurt by his departure, and I was too busy to even notice all of that. She was not a child any more.

"I am fine, baby. Why don't you go help your brothers with homework."

"But Mama, you really look tired."

And with those words spelt out I felt my water break.

"Aisha, call Hassan, send Abdul-Jabbar to fetch him from the *dukkan*. Hurry, hurry," I shouted.

Aisha ran like a crazy horse and in no time the whole team was here. Lulwa was crying in fear and Dana was trying to calm her down. Noor was laughing, thinking we were in the middle of one of her imaginary plays, and Abdurrahman looked pale. Mariam ran to hold my hand and along with Fatima carried me to the room. Aisha had already seen me deliver so many times that she knew exactly what to do.

"Fatima, get some towels. Abdurrahman, get a bucket and Mariam, help him fill it with warm water. Lulwa you stay with Noor, take her out of this room, and dry your tears there is nothing to cry about, Mama is having her baby. Dana, go look for a stick, something Mama can bite on."

She was so confident in every move she took. She was completely in control. She stood by me, helping me and calming me down until Hassan brought the midwife with him. Abdul-

Jabbar took the kids out of the room and Aisha managed to force Hassan out behind them.

"Hang on Mama, everything will be alright."

I wished my mama was here. I wondered if she was watching over me now, making sure I was fine and showering me with her strength. Layla was right there in front of my eyes staring back at me as though telling me that I could do it. I had done it many times before and this was my last. The more the pain increased, the more memories came back to me; I saw my whole life in two hours of labor.

"Mama, Mama, it is out I see the head," cried Aisha.

"Ma'am, give me one more push, come on, just one more," cried the midwife.

"Mama, a baby girl, a baby girl," screamed Aisha and rushed out to announce the arrival of the last member of our family.

The midwife gave me the baby all packed in her sheets. It was like yesterday when I had held my first-born and now eleven years later I was holding my last child.

"What will you name her?" asked Hassan.

I looked at her tiny eyes as they looked back at me and wondered how Mohammed could leave without seeing this angel born. She was so beautiful and actually had his face and I thought of calling her Amina for her grandmother but I didn't want anything to remind me of Mohammed at such a time. I thought of calling her so many names but nothing was as close to my heart, as meaningful to me as Layla.

"Layla, I want her to be Layla."

"Like your doll, Mama?" asked Noor.

"Like our doll, Layla. What do you think?"

She was the last and I knew she was going to be the spoilt one.

Just as everyone left me to rest I caught Aisha trying to hide her tears.

"What's wrong, Aisha?"

"Mama, why did he leave, why didn't he want us?"

"Baba?"

"Yes, Baba. The one we loved so much, the one we'd fight over who gets to sit on his lap. The one who used to make us laugh with his jokes and cry over his stories. Why Mama. What did we do wrong?"

"Nothing, baby. There are things I can't explain because I myself don't understand them. I know we were happy together and it was only when Hassan came that I heard things I am not sure are true. Have faith Aisha and be patient. Some day God will reward us for all that we are going through."

They loved their father and the most difficult times were the special occasions and celebrations when they remembered him. Seeing their newly born sister without her father around must have been a difficult thing for children to empathize with, to them it was simply unfair. It was an intricate time for me too. In all my deliveries Mohammed had always been there, he would never let me move an inch; he wanted to do everything himself even if it meant waking up for the baby just as long as he would see me rest. I missed my husband, as much as I was trying to hide my feelings or to forget the good times I couldn't deny missing him, his touch, his warmth, his love, his passion, everything. I wished I could hate him but I couldn't. I wished I had never met him, but how could I when I have learned so much from him.

"How lucky am I, Khadeeja? How lucky am I to have a beautiful young wife who loves me so much, a perfect mother to her children and a wonderful housekeeper. God must be pleased with me to give me you." I remembered him say once upon a time.

"It makes me feel good to know that you appreciate me. It makes me want to give more."

"Appreciate you? I love you, love you, love you."

I remembered his words so clearly as if they were just said to me. My face even turned red every time I hear myself repeating his words. How could such a relationship turn to a painful memory?

"Mohammed, I am pregnant again for the ninth time. My God how on earth are we supposed to take care of them all?"

"Ninth and tenth and eleventh time. The more children we have, the happier I will be. I want a whole soccer team, no, even more. I want a castle filled with kids running everywhere, with many rooms, and I want them to live with me forever, even after they marry. I want the boys to start a family business and I want the girls to go to school and learn from their amazing mother. I want to share so much with you, Khadeeja, so much is ahead of us and sometimes I even feel like time is running really slow."

Yeah, too slow until the time comes for you to leave me and the kids and look for your own future with another woman. If there was something I learned from my life with Mohammed, it would definitely be never believe a man. Never trust his words and build your dreams on them, and never wait for promises to be fulfilled. You will only hurt yourself that way.

*

Hassan walked in one day with a big wide smile on his face. He had a funny way of smiling, his eyes would open wide, his cheeks would turn red and you could see his teeth shining from a distance. He'd raise his eyebrows in such a way that you could only see a wrinkled forehead and his ears would turn so red that you could nearly feel their heat. He welcomed the children with delight, carrying them one after the other, throwing kisses everywhere. If you saw him that day you'd think he had found a treasure and I just couldn't wait to hear the news.

"What is it, what is it?" I ran behind him as he danced around the laughing and clapping kids.

"It's good news, Khadeeja, good news. Weren't you aching for any good news? Where is Aisha?"

"In the kitchen. Tell me what good news? Is Mohammed coming home?"

He frowned at the statement and gave me a look that made me feel so guilty for ruining his moment.

"Mohammed, Mohammed, Mohammed. Would you just forget about Mohammed for a second and hear the news I have for you."

"Tell me, I can't wait any more."

He took my hand hurriedly and pulled me behind him to the kitchen.

"Aisha, my lovely niece, the most beautiful girl in the world, would you leave us just a minute?" he said.

"What's going on, *khalo* Hassan, I have never seen you so happy before?" asked Aisha surprised.

"I am more than happy. You just go to your sisters and let me talk to your mother."

I couldn't wait any further so I started pushing her out of the kitchen so he'd give me the news. I jumped around him impatiently until finally he spelled out the unexpected.

"Khadeeja, there is a proposal, a marriage proposal."

"Marriage proposal? But Aisha has just entered her twelfth year. I can't possibly send her off at this age."

"First of all, you got married when you were only twelve. Second of all, it's not for Aisha, the proposal is for you."

That definitely was like a slap across my face. What has happened to Hassan, has he gone crazy? How can he say something like that, how can he even think of it? There was no way I could be with another man, not after Mohammed. Maybe it was easy for him to forget all about me, forget all that was between us and be with another woman, but I couldn't forget the past. I loved Mohammed as I always had. Even after he left me I couldn't hate him. I could still feel his warmth as if he was there next to me and there was something inside still hoping for his return. Mohammed was going to come back, someday he would realize his mistake and he would come back. I knew he would and it was all a matter of time.

At that moment I was so scared that I felt like running away from Hassan. What if he forces me to marry? Until finally God came to my rescue and I remembered that Mohammed never divorced me in the first place; he left without telling me anything.

"Hassan, you want a married woman to marry another man?"

"But you are not married any more."

"He never divorced me."

"You could ask for a divorce."

"Who told you that I want a divorce?"

"You have to get a divorce. Will you stay like this not knowing what to do with your life? Not divorced, not a widow but with no husband either?"

"Even if I got divorced I don't want to be with another man. I have seen enough from men."

"Khadeeja, my dear sister. This is a good man from a good family. He is well off and will take care of you and your nine children. Think of your children, think of their future. Do you want to work as a tailor all your life? This man will make you forget the past. You will be happy again. You deserve to be happy again."

"I am happy with what God had given me, Hassan. Please let's not talk about this any more. I don't want a divorce and my children will be well taken care off."

"That is selfish."

"Selfish? After all this time you call me selfish? Hassan, when I married Mohammed I was filled with fear. I begged Mama to keep me with her, I didn't want to leave but Mama wanted to see me happily married and in my own house before her death. I gave in not because I was convinced but because it was what Mama wanted. I thought I was going to be miserable. I thought my life would end but Mohammed proved me wrong. He was not only my husband he was my best friend, he was the father I never had and my family after Mama died. He was my world. I know this sounds crazy but he will come back, I know he will. As for the children, no human being can ever replace their father."

Hassan was disappointed. He didn't imagine that I would refuse such a proposal and I couldn't imagine how he brought such a proposal to me. A good man from a good family. Wasn't that what Mama said when she told me about my wedding in the first place? Well the good man from the good family deserted me and I can't even hate him for it. My God, what has happened to my life? Hassan was angry at me and guilt was haunting me. He was still young, he deserved to wed again and I know that he wouldn't even think of himself as long as the kids and I were alone. What should I do? I was in a really difficult situation and I couldn't be selfish.

As Hassan left the house Aisha, Mariam and Fatima walked in.

"Mama, what happened? We thought there was good news," said Mariam.

"No, baby, it wasn't good news after all. Maybe it was for Hassan, but your Mama saw it as bad news after all."

"What is it, Mama, please tell us," begged Aisha.

"Your uncle wants your mama to ask for a divorce so she can marry another man."

"What? Why? What if Baba came back?" screamed Mariam.

"No, Mama, don't do it, please. We don't want a new daddy please," cried Fatima.

Aisha though was silent. She tried to hold in her tears but failed to do so. Fatima and she were the most affected by what their father had done. They were the most who missed him for they had the most memories of their father.

"Don't worry, I won't do such a thing to you or your father. I love you children, you are my life and I won't do anything that might hurt you, and I promise to remain faithful to your father until the day I die."

And we hugged. The three of us were on the floor of the kitchen, crying and laughing at the same time, when Abdurrahman came running in.

"Hey, come quickly, come! Noor fell and she is crying. I don't know what happened there is blood everywhere."

I ran as fast as I could with the memory of Nader's accident haunting me and found my sweet Noor by the entrance stairs. Her leg was covered with blood and she cried so loudly she could hardly breathe.

"Baby what happened to you?"

All the children tried to explain but all I heard was perplexing mumbling. I examined her very quickly and the blood flow was very heavy. Abdul-Jabbar carried her and we rushed to the hospital.

The doctor took her right away; he knew Mohammed and remembered that he had seen me there once or twice. He told us that he had to do some stitching and asked us to wait outside. I was so worried; I started biting my fingernails as I was praying silently. Abdul-Jabbar would wipe my tears and hold my hand, trying to calm me down as I sat there trying to ignore the memories that came speeding up. It was the same as when I had been there before, eleven years ago; the hospital hadn't changed a bit. The aroma of the medicine was still nauseating, the dark corridors were claustrophobic and the courtyard was jammed with people. The more time Noor spent alone with the doctor, the more worried I got. The nurses walked in and out but no one said a thing to me.

"Khadeeja, what happened, where is Noor?" Hassan surprised me.

"She is in with the doctor. He said she needed stitching but a long time has passed, I don't know what is happening."

Hassan's face was pale and he couldn't wait for me to finish. He went to the door and knocked. The nurse opened it and he said something to her as she backed off and allowed him in. He came back in a few minutes and I was wondering why Noor wasn't with him.

"This naughty girl of yours broke her leg and they had to bandage it." he said.

"Where is she, I want to see her."

"Go ahead, the doctor is waiting for you."

Noor looked so innocent on the bed. She was only two years old and she seemed scared to death. Her eyes were red from crying and as soon as she saw me she started all over again. The doctor explained all that we had to do and the cast was to be removed in six weeks. Hassan carried her all the way home as he and Abdul-Jabbar sang to her to make her laugh again.

As we walked in the door there was another human being squeaking from hunger, Looloo.

"You should have left your breasts behind before you walked out!" cried Abdurrahman angrily as he slammed the door, while Mariam and Lulwa were giggling at his statement.

Aisha and Hassan placed Noor on the bed, the only bed we had, and all the kids were around her wondering what had happened. She was excited with all the attention she was getting. This one would get her water, that one would get her a sandwich. They would fight over who makes her laugh and who would read her a story. I have never seen her so happy before and I was glad it had all ended in a good way.

"I am sorry I screamed at you before, Khadeeja," said Hassan as he stood by the door.

"Come in, have some tea with me."

"What were you thinking of?"

"My life."

"What about it?"

"Nothing much. I was thinking of what it was and what it has become and what it could have been if Mohammed hadn't left."

"But he left."

"Hassan I beg you, let's not talk about this subject any more."

"I don't want to see you hurt."

"I am happy this way. I have a dream and this dream is what makes me wait for tomorrow. At night when the children have gone to sleep, the house chores are over and there is no more sewing I look at my door and wait for his arrival and when no one walks through the door then it's alright because there is always tomorrow."

"This is your dream? That he is going to come back?"

"This is my dream; that one day my knight, the only man for me, will come and take me from my pain and agony. He will carry me to wonderland where we will live happily ever after."

"It's a child's dream," laughed Hassan.

"Well you seem to forget something, Hassan."

"What is it? That you are slowly going insane."

"No, you have forgotten that after all I have been through, I am still a child."

*

"Mama, I dreamt of a ring made of gold. A wide ring, and an old woman was giving it to me. She looked kind and beautiful and I wanted to put it on but the woman stopped me and said 'not yet, soon, but not yet,'" said Aisha.

She was thirteen years old and beautiful, very attractive, very intelligent. Many proposed from when she was eleven but I wanted her to finish her education, which was only thirteen years for girls at the time. Aisha matured early. Being the oldest of her brothers and sisters made her grow up fast, specially as her father left and I had to work. She learned to take on much of the house chores and responsibilities. She was a shy young girl, tall and thin. Her hair was long and always neatly braided. Her lips still had its raspberry color and her tanned skin was soft as silk. I saw Mama in her. She had her beauty, her confidence, her intelligence. May God bless her, for she suffered so much for her age.

"Hassan, I had a visit from someone today. A woman asking for Aisha," I told Hassan.

"In marriage?"

"Yes."

"And you are actually telling me about this one. Interesting, you have sent away all the rest. How come?" he asked surprised.

"Aisha is not a child any more. She has finished her schooling and is capable of being a good wife and mother now."

"And you like this woman?"

"She seemed nice. I haven't asked about the family yet. I wanted you to know about it first and tell me how you feel about it."

"Do you want me to send for her father?"

"No, well I don't know, you do what you think is right. As for the proposal, you were her father more than he ever was, so your decision matters to me."

"Who are they?"

"They come from Persia originally but have lived in Bahrain since childhood. His name is Hamid Alabdulla. His mother told me that he worked in Saudi Arabia for five years and just found a job here in Bahrain in Mina Salman port as an engineer."

"Let me send a letter to Aziz, see if he knows Mohammed's whereabouts. Her father is still alive after all, and we have to respect that no matter what she is still his daughter. At the same time I will ask about him and see what I find."

I asked for some time from Bibi Gul, Hamid's mother, and waited in patience for Mohammed's letter which didn't take long to arrive.

Dear brother Hassan,
I have received a letter from brother Aziz about my daughter Aisha's marriage proposal and I trust you with my daughter. If you see that her husband will treat her well, be good to her, and give her what she deserves then may God be with them.

I only discovered now that you have left your work to join Khadeeja and the children and I truly apologize for ruining so many lives. Please do let me know about any marriage details and do let me know if you need anything.
Thank you
Mohammed

It was a letter I had memorized for I made Aisha read it to me more than a hundred times, over and over and over again. Hassan only heard the best about Hamid and the last step, the most difficult for me, was asking Aisha. I tried to recall all that I had shared with Mama on my wedding memories, the *jihaz*, what she told me about marriage and all that stuff.

"Khadeeja, I know you are used to my protection but you have to learn how to rely on yourself. Be sure that I won't give you to just anyone, you are more precious to me than anything in this world. The man I chose to wed you is a good man. He is old enough to take care of you, he is educated and well off. You were wanted by many, Khadeeja, but I chose the best and you are to get married this Thursday."

How should I trust a man to take care of my daughter, my first-born? There was something inside me that told me she was safer with me and there was another thing that told me let her marry him, don't be unfair and over protective. Her happiness is not to be locked up in the house but her happiness was to have a family of her own, to be with a man and fall in love, to be a mother someday. I had no choice but to call her in to the room and pray that I was only doing the right thing.

"Yes, Mama?"

My God, she was so angelic, I couldn't stop staring at her beauty, how much my little baby grew up. It was as if we just met after a very long separation, as if I haven't seen her for such a long time.

"Aisha, come sit next to me, we have so much to talk about."

"Is there something wrong?"

"No baby, but I need to tell you something concerning only you. Remember the woman who came to visit me two weeks ago, Bibi Gul? Well she was here asking for your hand."

"I know, Mama. I heard her talk to you while I was preparing the tea. Besides, I was reading Baba's letter to you a thousand times a day."

"And?"

"I have been thinking about it since that time and at first I was really scared but I am ready, and I don't want to spend the rest of my life here. Don't get offended, Mama, you know I love you and our little home, but I am ready to move on. I know I am ready and all my friends are getting married."

"You are a good girl, Aisha, but don't do anything for me or for your uncle. If you want to marry you have to be sure that you are doing it for yourself. Marriage is not easy. You saw how happy Baba and I were and in a blink of an eye everything changed. I am not saying that the same thing will happen to you, nor am I trying to scare you, but I want you to be prepared, life is full of surprises."

"I know, Mama. If you say this man is good enough than let it be."

I couldn't believe my little daughter was speaking to me with so much confidence and maturity. She knew exactly what she wanted and she was all ready to face whatever was waiting for her. I looked at Layla sitting on my bed, still wondering if it was the right thing to do, and she seemed to stare back with a smile telling me it will turn out just fine, better than I had ever hoped for.

★

"My first born is getting married," Mohammed told Abdulghafar, his best friend in Dubai, "Aisha is getting married, and I can't believe that."

It's been a long time since Mohammed had left them and though he had a different life he was never able to forget his real family. He was married, a rich wife, three children. He should be happy. He wanted to be happy but he couldn't. Deep in his heart he knew that his wife was nothing like Khadeeja, these children didn't even have half the beauty, intelligence and manners his children had. He had a lot, more than he had previously had but he had lost even more. He'd lost a beautiful home, a kind smile when he woke up, a shy kiss before he slept. He missed Khadeeja's humor, her spirit, her love that filled the air. He missed everything about her, everything.

Nothing was the same any more. He married for money and his new wife knew that. She knew it so well that she had to remind him of it every day.

"Don't forget who you were and where you came from, and what I made out of you. Don't forget that all of this is mine, you are mine, I bought you and I could sell you anytime," she would say.

He knew Khadeeja would never say that even if she really had bought him with her money. She was too decent, too beautiful to say that.

He would sit in his (or actually her) luxurious house in Jumeira, Dubai staring out from the bedroom window thinking of Khadeeja; what did she do, how did she manage?

"She must be so beautiful now, her long black hair over her shoulders, her smile filling the house with joy. The children must be wonderful young men and women by now." He would whisper in the dark, "Do they hate me? Do they remember me? Will they ever forgive me?"

He has always expected a letter to come from Khadeeja's brothers asking for the divorce papers. Such a beautiful lady must want to get married again, and it wouldn't be fair to keep her hanging on. When the letter came from Aziz he was almost sure that it was the request he had dreaded for so long, but to his surprise it was his first-born's wedding, it was a happy letter.

He could remember clearly the day Khadeeja brought Aisha to this world. He remembered rushing to get the midwife, the ladies outside waiting for the news. He remembered Aunty Jameela and her funny comments. But most of all he remembered how beautiful Khadeeja was holding her baby. How delicate and graceful was her touch. She was a baby mother and this mother was letting go of her baby, our baby, who had grown up to be a wonderful bride. He wished he could be there, he wished he hadn't left, all he could do now was write a letter that would give away his daughter, his own flesh and blood, in a piece of paper, just some paper and ink. He knew that life was slowly punishing him for what he had done.

★

There was hardly any time left for the wedding to take place. Hassan worked harder to make sure Aisha would get a good *jihaz* ready for her and I started sewing what would be her wedding *thoubs*. The *jihaz* for Aisha was very different from my *jihaz*. Aisha no longer wanted it to be mainly *thoubs* but wanted more dresses that were now fashionable for girls to wear. It was a big step for me to allow my daughter to wear a two piece suit that showed the ankles and almost half of the arms, if not all.

"No, no, no, you will not go to your husband's house in that!" I screamed one day.

"But Mama, everyone wears them now, all my friends, my neighbors and everyone in school."

"What do you want the people to say about me, Aisha? Khadeeja couldn't raise a well-mannered girl? I will not tolerate people talking about us, I have heard enough already."

"But Mama!"

"That's enough go to your room and we'll see."

It was only through Hassan that I finally got convinced. Maybe I shouldn't be so strict. Maybe she was right; the world was changing and we had to accept it there wasn't anything I could do about it. It was enough that there wasn't much I could give her, just some jewelry, some hair accessories. I also had my wedding slippers that she didn't want; "Very old, Mama. People will laugh at me." she would say.

If Mama was alive she would have never allowed her granddaughter to go to her husband's house with so little. She would've wanted to give her bags filled with silk and embroidered *thoubs*, like the ones she gave me. She would've dressed her up from head to toe with jewelry and precious stones. She would have given her cutlery made of pure silver and bathed her with rich incense specially brought to her from India. Mama would've given her so many things but all I could give her now was my blessing.

The first day, as it is my day, was the announcement day, but there were not many to tell. The doors that were open for my announcement have been closed on our faces for a long time now. Aisha got to invite her friends and I told some of those who I tailored for. Hassan asked me to invite his friends' wives and a few neighbors and that was it, the house would have not carried more than that anyway. There was no need for Aisha to dress up, no one was going to show up anyway and so we celebrated quietly at home and had a memorable time together.

The following days were simple too. Some of my family members came to help out with the decorations and Aunty Jameela, an old woman now, brought many gift with her for Aisha.

"It's like I am seeing my sister getting married all over again," she said.

During the fourth day Aisha had to dress up. Her sisters Fatima and Mariam, along with her friends, were helping her as I was out welcoming the neighbors and family who came to see the gifts coming in from the husband's family. The house was too small yet it was beautifully decorated with jasmine, *mashmoum*, and palm tree leaves. I had placed a chair in the center of the room for Aisha and arranged the *misnad* in a way that won't make her as suffocated as I was on that day.

"Come on, Khadeeja, the gifts are already here. Where is Aisha?" Aunty Jameela said hurriedly.

"I will go get her. Just entertain the guests with whatever you have."

I walked into Aisha's room and found her hiding behind the curtains.

"What's wrong, baby, are you afraid?" I asked, worriedly remembering myself on my wedding day.

"Oh no, no, I am just hiding from you. It's a surprise, Mama. Please wait for me outside, I want you to see me when I am all ready."

"Well hurry, everyone is waiting."

Just as I walked out I saw Fatima and Mariam running in with more jasmine and I just hoped they were not going to make a fool out of themselves and me.

"Here she comes, here she comes," I heard one of Aisha's friends scream in excitement.

And my baby walked in all dressed in red. I have never seen such beauty in my life. Her eyes were dazzling, her skin was shining and she carried the smile of a royal. Her hair was flowing with every move and her body swayed and she walked in perfect steps. Her smile had dignity and her confidence filled the room with every move. I was proud and I wished Mama was alive to see how her granddaughter, the one named after her, had grown to be.

As Aisha took her seat the gifts came in. This time there were no trays; instead they used silver decorated carts, small carts with glass and stones. There were only three of them. The first was filled with textiles, silk and velvet. The second cart had boxes of jewelry and oil incense, and the third was the dowry. The dowry was twenty gold coins neatly placed in a golden box.

I watched Aisha's happy face as I remembered my own gift-receiving day. I had six trays filled with so much stuff that I thought would make me the happiest girl in the world. Mama was proud, the guests were envious and I couldn't wait to meet Mohammed. Funny how life forces you to live in so many illusions.

The girls went to show off their sister's stuff as I started getting ready for another day, a hectic and difficult day. Hamid's family were coming over and I had to fix them a big fiesta. I spent all night and next morning cooking while the girls did the cleaning, and in no time the guests were already arriving.

Bibi Gul started introducing her family one by one but they were too many to memorize all at once. They all talked at the same time and I was with them in body only, for my mind was drifting in many directions. They seemed simple and nice, but was my baby going to be happy with them? I still didn't know if I was doing the right thing and my Layla was the only one who seemed to encourage me to go on.

They were religious and I was scared that Aisha's dresses were going to be a scandal. They were a bit old fashioned and had a funny accent. Bibi Gul was a good person though. Just before they left she took me on a side and tried to ease my tension up a bit.

"Listen, Khadeeja, I know you went through really difficult times in your life and have killed yourself to protect your children from going through what you had to go through, but rest assure, Khadeeja, that Hamid is a good man, he fears God and won't do anything to hurt Aisha. Don't worry, I give you my word and God is my witness," she told me.

"Oh, Bibi Gul, thank you so much. It's just that this is my first child to wed and she had helped me with so many things, it's difficult to see her go."

"Don't worry, Khadeeja. Hamid found a house right by the corner. It's a two floor house and he wanted to take a floor and rent the second. Then he changed his mind and asked me to come live with him. But Khadeeja, I have a house of my own and I am comfortable enough, so I was thinking how about you moving in there with them."

That came to me as a surprise. I never imagined such an offer but I didn't want anyone's pity.

"Bibi Gul thank you, but we are fine here really."

"Hamid will leave it open for anyone to come and you wouldn't want any strangers living there. It's just inconvenient you know, sharing one entrance and using one staircase, one rooftop, one attic, you see the picture?"

"Well I won't promise anything, but let me talk to my brother and we'll let you know as soon as we decide."

"It was a good gathering, Khadeeja. Thank you very much. We are lucky to have people like you as in-laws."

"Same here, Bibi Gul, same here."

The house was finally empty and the girls were busy cleaning up. Hassan, who was in the men's wedding, walked in and immediately started bothering the girls and looking for the boys. He was happier about Aisha's wedding than I was and his constant smile only added more wrinkles to his tanned face.

"I am hungry, did the women finish all the food?"

"Uncle, whom do you think we invited, barbarians? Of course there is food," said Dana.

"Then shut that hole in your face and feed your starving uncle."

"We have loads of food, how do I know what you want to eat?"

"Don't be so stingy, get me everything!"

The girls started to laugh and I was finally able to sit down and rest for a while. Hassan started dancing around and boys imitated him. Laughter filled the air and another party started. Dana shouted for help and objected to the idea that they all got to play and have fun without her. Hassan went to fetch his food tray and I decided to call it a day and retire. I was just getting into bed when I heard a loud crash. I ran outside into where the children were and found them giggling as they looked at the flipped tray, broken glass, and scattered food all over the room that I had cleaned only moments earlier. I looked at them and felt the boiling blood in my angry face. I knew it was Hassan. I took a quick look around me but couldn't find him. I walked out and noticed the door moving slightly. I ran back in and there he was hiding behind the door like a child. He was trying to make a joke out of it but I forced him to clean the entire room all by himself and went back into my room. To be honest. I couldn't stop laughing the minute I shut the door behind me. Hassan had a way with everything even when it came to running away from trouble just like little children do.

I couldn't sleep for Bibi Gul's offer was still on my mind. I walked out to check on the children and found them all sitting around Hassan who was reading them a story.

"Hide, the monster is here, she will swallow us with her fiery anger!" he screamed, as he saw me and the children screamed behind him.

"Oh come on now, I am not a monster. You were naughty and I had to punish you."

"Mama is a princess, Mama is a princess," they all chanted together.

"Hassan, I have to speak to you."

"Go ahead I am all ears."

"Alone, please come to the room. And children, look what time it is, shouldn't you all be in bed now?"

"Don't worry, Mama I will put them to bed. You can go with *khalo* Hassan."

I walked into my room followed by Hassan and I didn't know how to start the subject. I didn't want to offend him and I knew that this was a very sensitive subject. Hassan was a good man but also a very quick-tempered man. I looked at his soothing eyes and held his aging hand towards the mattress. We sat down and I could clearly see how his smiley face had transformed into a serious one, a concerned one.

"Bibi Gul gave me an offer today. Hamid has a two floor house that he owns. He will be taking one floor and the second is the offer."

"Pity... After all these years, Khadeeja, you want me to accept such a thing?"

"She said that we were better than strangers who will be sharing..."

"No, Khadeeja. You want a house, I will sell the *dukkan* and buy you a house but I will not accept such an offer."

He left the house angrily as Noor and Layal came running into my arms. He never wanted anyone's pity. His dignity was as it had been in the good days when Mama was alive and he had a good job in Dubai, it was as if he denied the fact that we were now poorer than the poor. How could I open such a subject with him? How selfish of me to think of myself and the children when Hassan gave up his own life to give us a decent one? It was the fact that we would be saving the rent which kept increasing every year that probably made me forget how such a thing would hurt my brother.

I stayed wide awake waiting for him, regretting opening such a subject with him. It was after the morning prayers when I finally saw him walk into the house. He looked beat and tired and came straight towards me. He took my hands, kissed them and wished me a good night and went into his bedroom. I woke Abdurrahman up to work instead of his uncle in the *dukkan* and went to get some sleep myself.

*

As the other nights, the henna night passed by quickly. Aisha was gorgeous in her green *thoub* and her friends and sisters surrounded her while being decorated with henna. She looked happy, my little baby, she wasn't scared or anxious as I was but very calm and excited. Maybe I was doing the right thing after all; maybe she wasn't as young and inexperienced as I thought she was.

And finally the big night was here. Aisha was very busy all day and I was with Bibi Gul in Hamid's house where the wedding was going to take place. We had to neatly organize the seating using as much space as possible and arrange the area where the bride was going to sit. Bibi Gul had hired a professional singer and the caterer came all the way from Persia. The food was already coming in and Hamid had ordered boxes and boxes of fresh fruits for the occasion that had to be washed and placed in baskets ready to be served. The nuts were brought from Iran as a gift from Bibi Gul's distant relative and the *samboosa* filled the room with a delicious aroma. By the time I could leave to freshen up and get ready, Aisha was almost ready herself and as before refused to let me see her. She always loved surprises, always loved to dress up with my clothes and use my jewelry and make-up and amaze me with her beauty when she's all done. She has always been her father's little princess, he made her feel like a royal, dress like a royal, and he was her king. It was too bad that when he left he was transformed into the villain, a monstrous villain who ruined her beautiful fairy tale. And here she is, a princess again, all ready to leave and start off on her own, with her prince, the prince she had been dreaming about for so long. Never before had I been so proud.

The guests were already arriving and the girls were busy singing and dancing until it was time for Aisha's arrival. With every beat of the drum my heart sank deeper. With every note sung a tear came running until I finally saw her, my little angel. Her steps were like those of a queen. Her white dress, which I gave her as a gift, was such a perfect fit that showed her mature body. She was so beautiful and I knew Mama was proud of her. Her sisters were in tears, her friends were clapping in joy, her in-laws were overjoyed. As she took her seat she gave me a long grateful look that left me speechless and on the verge of crying like a child, and I knew she was happy, I had done the right thing for her, look at her, she is all grown up and ripe, ready to seize the day.

Everyone seemed to have a wonderful time. Dinner was delicious and the small space didn't seem to be a problem at all. People were leaving early though, but that was normal when the wedding takes place in the groom's house. We were the only ones left, the girls, Bibi Gul and I, and Aisha was about to enter her room where she would be waiting for her husband to join her.

"Mama, thank you for everything. I am very happy, Mama, please don't worry about me. Don't be sad, I will be just fine."

"You have my blessings, baby, I will pray for your happiness. Be a good wife, Aisha. Love your husband and allow him to love you back. Be a good friend to him for such friendship helps a marriage."

"I wish we had time alone, Mama, just you and me, to talk before I left."

"Yes baby, but we still have so much to share. We are literally neighbors." I laughed, trying to ease the moment. I didn't want to cry, not now, not in front of her, not in her happiest moment.

"I love you, Mama. I love you for being so good to us, for all your sacrifices and hard work."

"I love you too, baby, go now, for we must leave before Hamid comes."

And my first baby left my nest to build her own. What a beautiful feeling, yet difficult at the same time. I couldn't think of anything at the time but I heard myself whispering to the moon, "Oh, Mohammed, you missed watching your dream come true, our Aisha is a woman now, the most beautiful woman in the world."

★

It was one of his many lonely nights; Amina, Mohammed's wife, was in a neighborhood gathering and the children were busy with their own lives. Mohammed sat wondering at the stars. The moon stared back, blaming him for what he had put himself into. The sky was as black as it was the night he left.

"But Mama, I don't want to sleep," he heard a neighbor's child cry.

"Come here, child; let me sing you a lullaby. Tomorrow is a new day and you can play as much as you want to," his mother replied.

He heard the mother's voice and his heart ached with memory, the memory of his Khadeeja as she sang to her little ones, their little ones. She would hold them to her breast and rock them gently until they slept. He heard her kiss them and read a verse from the Quran, followed by a small prayer before she would run to his arms and bury her beautiful face in his chest.

It was at that moment when he remembered his wife's last pregnancy. Yes, Mohammed had left when she was pregnant. He placed his hand on his aching heart and cried. He wished he could throw his heart away, far away from here so he'd stop feeling guilty. She must have delivered now, that was for sure. He wondered if it was a boy or a girl. He knew it was beautiful for all his children were, they took their mother's beauty.

"Forgive me, Nader," he whispered to the sky, "forgive me."

He felt him watching; his dead son was watching from heaven. He knew he must be ashamed of his father. He knew he must be angry at him for leaving his mother. But he also knew that he has been watching the whole time, so he must know why he left in the first place. He must excuse him. He would understand and forgive him, maybe even help him by praying for him.

And he cried, he cried himself to sleep as Khadeeja cried herself to sleep for many years, each aching for the other, each longing for each other's touch, each praying for a better future.

Chapter Nine

"Khadeeja, what would you do if I was suddenly gone?" Hassan surprised me one day.

"Why, Hassan, you want to leave?"

"No this is my home now, there is no where else to go to."

"Then what made you ask such a ridiculous question?"

"Nothing. You know me, always with weird questions, but tell me what would you do?"

"Hassan, go to your *dukkan*, I am not in the mood for your jokes."

"Okay then, if you need anything you know where to find me."

Hassan left with heavy footsteps. It was the first time that he didn't feel like going to work.

"Let me sleep today Khadeeja, let someone else hold my *dukkan*," he told me when I woke him up earlier.

"There is no one here today; the boys are in school and you know it's their finals. Come on, Hassan, don't be a lazy dog now."

I wish I hadn't forced him to go that day. I didn't know he was really tired, I thought he was just being lazy, nothing more. The weather was extremely hot and the humidity took your breath away. I was busy in the kitchen when I heard the door knocking very roughly and loudly.

"Open the door ma'am, open the door quickly, Hassan is sick."

"Hassan? What happened to Hassan, where is he?" I ran to open the door as my heart nearly popped out. The sun's bright rays were making it even more difficult to see what was going on. All I could grasp was two men carrying Hassan who lay motionless between their arms. I opened his room and watched the men place him on the bed.

"What happened?" I asked them.

"Ma'am, Brother Hassan lost consciousness in the *dukkan*. We found him like that and rushed him home as you see while one of the other men went to bring the doctor."

"My God, is he okay? Will he be fine?"

"Don't worry," said one of them, "could you please lend us a fan? It might help him a bit."

As I went to fetch the fan with trembling legs I heard a second knock on the door. It was the doctor with a third stranger.

"Yes, doctor, do come in," I managed to say.

"Would you please leave us alone?" he said as he walked into Hassan's room.

Without even thinking I ran as quickly as I could, taking with me Noor and Looloo to Aisha's house to call her before the doctor left. I was too scared of being alone with strangers like that and if I was lucky Hamid would be at home and he could do something. I couldn't believe that our strong Hassan was sick. I couldn't believe how much I needed Mohammed that moment.

"Aisha, come quickly, Hassan is ill. He fainted and they carried him home. The doctor is with him and I don't know what to do, Aisha, please come quickly." I was having a panic attack and frightened Aisha even more. She was moving quickly all around trying to fetch everything at once, her slippers, her *abaya*, even her husband whom I was glad was around.

"Hamid, Hamid, wake up please, it's an emergency," I heard her yell and in no time we were all running home with two giggling children thinking we were playing catch with them.

The doctor was leaving the room as we walked in. He looked pale and I feared the worst. He took Hamid aside and they talked for a few minutes and left. The men left with him and Hamid looked confused.

"What, Hamid? Will he be fine?" I asked.

"*Khala* Khadeeja, please sit down," he said softly.

"Why, I want to go see my brother, Hamid, say something, what did the doctor tell you?"

"Aisha please, come sit with your mother."

I knew there was bad news but I didn't expect to hear that kind of news. Hamid's words came very slowly and heavily and he was struggling to find a good way to tell us what the doctor told him.

"It's going to be really difficult for me to say this but I'm afraid I have to. *Khalo* Hassan died of a heart attack, may he rest in peace. I am sorry."

It seemed like the words had slapped me across the face as so many words have done before and I couldn't believe him at first, but when I broke in to the room and saw Hassan stiff and cold I felt death running through my veins. I couldn't stop thinking of his last words before he left that day. "What would you do if I was suddenly gone?" Hassan knew he was going to die, somehow he knew. Was he sick? Was there something he was hiding? Why did I force him to go to work? Why do all men leave me in this sudden way? What have I done to deserve all this?

I had lost a person very dear to my heart and I felt miserable. When Mama died I never thought I would ever be so sad again but with Hassan's death I proved myself wrong. I even grieved for Mama all over again. I had to write to Aziz to tell him and he arrived two days later. His wife came too, along with his older son, Abdullah, named after Baba of course.

"Khadeeja, I am so sorry. What happened? Why didn't you tell me he was sick?" said Aziz.

"He wasn't, well maybe he wasn't, he didn't feel like going to the *dukkan*, I made him wake up and he listened to me, he went to work. We both thought it was only laziness, at least, I did. After only a couple of hours he was brought in and when the doctor came he was already gone," I cried.

"Okay, I will take care of the funeral and you try to contact his wife."

"His wife? My God, Aziz, do you even know anything about us any more? Haifa died a long time ago. Why do you think Hassan was here the whole time? You think he walked out on his wife too? It's like we don't have the same blood running through our veins. You know what, I am really sorry I called you. Please leave right away. I will take care of everything. Hassan and I never needed your help before, we won't need it now," I screamed, and walked out the room.

I meant every word I said to Aziz. Even in our desperate times when Hassan, the kids and I were nearly thrown out of the house for not paying the rent, Aziz insisted in selling Mama's house and took his share instead of letting us stay there. And this wife of his. Why didn't she show up when Mama died? Where was she when Mama was sick?

"Aunty Khadeeja?"

"Who is it?"

"It's me, may I come in?"

Abdullah walked into my room holding Looloo's hand. I could tell they were already friends, which was weird in a way because Looloo didn't like strangers. I asked him to come in and have a seat next to me and to tell you the truth, I was glad I met my first nephew.

"Aunty Khadeeja, please don't get angry with Baba," he said gently.

"I am not angry with him, I don't know him, to me he is a stranger."

"You know if he had the chance to change the past he would."

"It's a bit too late for that now isn't it."

"You can start over again."

"I don't think so, Abdullah, you are too young to understand."

"You know, *khala* Khadeeja, I am glad I met you. We will be leaving tomorrow, Mama doesn't want to stay and as usual Baba does what she says."

"Yeah, well, he lost his own family for that you know."

"I know, but I don't want to be like him. I want to stay in touch with you, that is if you don't mind, of course. Since I have arrived I have seen unconditional love all around. I have seen what a family is really all about. I never felt that way before, you know."

"Of course, Abdullah. You are my nephew and I love you. I am sorry I welcomed you all this way but losing Hassan destroyed me and I don't know what to do now. I would love to write to you and you are always welcome here."

I felt guilty. Maybe I was too harsh after all, but reality was too harsh on me too. I should have tried to be more welcoming, at least with my nieces and nephews. Maybe Aziz's wife had a good reason for not attending the funeral. Maybe living in Dubai wasn't as easy as I had thought. But Mama treated her like her own daughter. She was always welcomed in our house yet it was her decision to resist us. She wanted Aziz for herself, only herself and no one else. I tried to convince myself that she wasn't so bad after all but truth spoke differently. And here comes Abdullah, all grown up, realizing how unfair his parents had been towards us. How dare I turn my back on him?

★

Aziz and his family left the following day after the funeral and the only good thing I had from his coming was meeting Abdullah. There was so much I had to think of now that Hassan was gone. I knew I couldn't afford the rent and the *dukkan* had to be closed down. The boys were still very young and in school and asking one of them to sacrifice his education to work in the *dukkan* wouldn't be fair. I couldn't work there either it was a disgrace; a woman in the market, selling goods, dealing with men, I would embarrass my children. The whole society would shut them off. I couldn't do such a thing to them. Maybe I should sell it and see where that would take me, or maybe Hamid had a better idea of running it. I didn't know what to do. My Hassan died and my heart died with him, but it's when you think the whole world had just turned its back on you that God finds the perfect solution.

Chapter Ten

I felt like there was no running away from reality and I only found myself with my *abaya* and a very exigent idea, Mecca.

"I am going to Mecca." I found myself saying.

"With who?" cried Aisha.

"Aunty Jameela went with this group once and she was very happy with their services. They were cheap too."

"But Mama, you can't go alone."

"Please, Aisha, I need to go. I need a break from everything and there is no better place to hide for a while. You have to understand that I need this really badly."

"I will ask Hamid if he could lend you some money," said Aisha, defeated. She was worried, I could tell from the way she looked at me. She too had lost so much; her brother, her father, and now her uncle. I knew she was worried about me, worried about losing me, worried that I might just walk out on them, but I had to go, not only for myself but for their sakes as well. I knew that such a place would heal my soul and I would return to them full of energy and optimism. Yes, I couldn't afford it, but Aisha didn't know that I had sold my hair; my long black hair was all gone, cut short for the trip to Mecca. I had to hide it under my scarf of course, so no one would notice. Only Layla new my secret, she was the only one I could trust with it.

"If you do such a thing I will never speak to you again. I have saved some money and I am pretty sure it will do."

"Well if you insist, then don't forget to pray for me. Don't worry about anything, Fatima and I will take care of it all."

And I went. I went with a group of women, all older than I was, and our leader was a sheikh from a neighboring village with a couple of men who helped us around. We took a boat from Bahrain to Saudi Arabia and then went by bus from Dammam through Riyadh and Jeddah until, finally, Mecca. As we arrived the weather was just perfect, the sun was setting and the humidity was unusually low. The men wore their *ehram* which was a towel-like garment, and the women were either in their *abaya*s or in a white *thoub* with white *hijabs*. The children wore white as well and looked very angelic, truly God's angels, and I wished I had brought one of the girls with me. If only I had the money.

As we entered the city it was time for the evening prayers. The roads ahead were empty as people were busy getting ready to pray and the call to the prayer seemed to echo throughout the country. It was a special time in every Muslim heart. It was one of the things I had missed from my old house, the call to the prayers from the neighborhood mosque, but hearing it in Mecca was a different experience. It was more like a call to the heart and I couldn't stop the tears from flowing. I could see the mosque, the harem, where the Ka'aba was as we drove closer. It seemed to shine from where it stood, with birds flying all around and children playing by the entrance gates. The manara, which is a tower-like extension, stood proud and tall, watching over millions of devout Muslims walking in and out spiritually filled with faith. The marble building had a sparkling effect that was somehow magnetic and the grand doors seemed like opened arms welcoming you to the land of paradise. You simply can't not get attached to such a place. In here you can throw all your problems away, you can sit back and talk to God forever, not that you can't anywhere else, but this place has its magic sprinkling every where. You feel angels are all around you, you feel safe, protected, loved. There is no peace like that found anywhere but in Mecca.

The men stayed separately from the women even though it was an open, spacious mosque. I didn't know where to sit until a little Indonesian kid came pulling my *abaya* towards where some older Indonesians were, and even though I couldn't understand a word they said, they wanted me to sit with them. Thanks to sign language, the mother managed to explain that if they squeezed in we'd all manage to pray. It was an amazing location as well. The Ka'aba was right in front of me and I was away from the crowd. Maqam Ibrahim which was the rock Prophet Ibrahim stood on while building the Ka'aba, and so had his foot prints, was to my right and I could also see the entrance to Zamzam well, where the grounds exploded with water for Prophet Ibrahim's wife, Hajar who was Ismael's mother and left abandoned in the desert.

I loved watching the expressions on people's faces here in the Harem. People tend to forget who they were, show their real selves with no masks on, as if they were no longer on this planet. They go in to a deep sense of meditation so that they feel nothing of what's going on around them. No evil exists in this place, no hatred or anger; for once you don't feel the devil around. It's simply heaven.

I cherished this place. I remember Mama praying to see the Ka'aba once and I remember Mohammed promising to take me there. Hassan came here one time, a long time ago with Baba, before I was even born, and he too promised to take me some day. I never thought I'd be lonely. I never thought that so much pain existed in this world. Was I asking for too much, I wondered, was it too much to seek for what I wanted most, the real thing, the stuff that helps you wake up in the morning and face a new day, the stuff that pulls you up to your feet and gives you hope and strength? All I wanted was some happiness, some security. I missed so much in my life; all the things that I grew up around were not there any more. I was lonely.

Being here helped my soul rest for a little while. I could sit back and whisper anything that came to mind with no second thoughts, with no fear, with no regrets. It was like being in Mama's arms again, that type of security. When I was there I knew no one would hurt me, just like a little baby that crawls to her Mama's arms. I look at the Ka'aba and I feel it talking to me. It might be funny, it might be crazy, but I know that it had empathy towards me. It somehow embraced me with its light and it was the kind of embrace that I needed. I wish I could stay there forever. I wish I always felt that secure.

The next stop was Al Medina Al Munawara, the Prophet's land, after spending ten days in Mecca. That was another four-hour drive but a beautiful one, really memorable. The men had drums and we were singing Islamic songs all the way. The children even had their own special contributions from things they learned in school. It was a drive through the mountains and desert and how amazing when one thinks of the Prophet

Mohammed's days when the journey from Mecca to Medina was made on foot. How much he, PBUH, had to go through to spread our religion and get us to where we are now. It was on these lands that the word of God was spread; it was on these lands that the first Islamic wars took place, and they witnessed the first Islamic–Jewish negotiations. How precious and holy are these lands.

The moment I entered the Prophet's land I felt a shiver in my body, I felt as if the air was hugging me and the vibe filled my heart and soul with love and faith. Everything was different everything was better; the life, the harmony, the land, even the fruits, the dates, the vegetables. The sun was cooler, the moon had a special shine, and the stars had a continuous twinkle. The people were helpful and welcoming and their homes were open for visitors from all over the world.

The most beautiful scene was the green *quba* of the Medina harem. It stood proud and strong on the marble building surrounded with the minarets from all around. The *quba* marked the Prophet's grave location which lay directly underneath. No one could see the actual grave, even from the inside of the mosque, only selected men were privileged to enter the room. All that could be seen was the room walls, said to be *Sayeda* Aisha's, one of his wives' house where he died. There was a specific time for women to visit the area and pray in the *rawdha*, which was an area between the grave and the *minbar*, where the prophet prayed known to be part of heaven. I wish I could explain how I felt in the harem. As I looked towards the room the whole world seemed to disappear around me. The ladies pushing left and right, the unbearable heat, the screams of crying children and the enchantment of prayers were lost in complete peace and silence. The golden room gates were shining with faith. The floors were ever more spiritual. The air was filled with a heavenly aroma. It was just me and him, the prophet, PBUH. I cried. I wanted to complain, I wanted to spell out all my troubles, all my pain but I cried. I cried for my mama, I cried for Nader, I cried for Mohammed, for Hassan, even for Baba whom I wished was alive this time to protect me more than anything else. And I felt him there, Prophet Muhammad, listening to every word said by my tears, understanding each and every unspoken sentence. He was there to comfort me, to give me strength and to remind me of God's reward. I know he was there, I felt him there. And he made a new person out of me. Yes it was truly heaven. I almost forgot my own children in that place, such a breathtaking experience.

And all of a sudden there was this feeling of contentment. I was strong again and there was a smile on my face. I walked towards the grand mosque doors and as I left I felt a happy wind blowing against my bare face, and raindrops ran against my cheeks. I knew God had answered my prayers, I knew the Prophet accepted my visit and I was relieved. I was ready to return and finish my journey, difficult yet rewarding.

On our way back to Mecca our group leader took us to Uhud Mountain where the Uhud battle took place and where the martyrs were buried. Standing between the mountain and the graveyard was so symbolic, and as I heard the story I saw my own life with all its pain and sadness, nothing compared to what our Prophet and his followers went through. You see the graves marking their heroism and you think, what am I next to those great people? I wished Hassan was buried here, I wished Hassan had died the way they died so I would know that he was in heaven with no doubt. But I thanked God anyway and prayed for my children, my grandchildren and for myself.

It was the most magnificent two weeks of my life and returning was rather sad. If it weren't for my children I would have tried to stay even longer. The journey back was difficult; the bus stopped in the middle of the way and we had to wait in the sun for five hours till someone came to help. I was seasick all the way to Bahrain and by the time I reached home I had a fever and a bad cold. But at the end it was good to be home.

This was my first trip, but a trip that crammed my heart with faith. I realized that no person will ever see happiness unless he is filled with faith, only then will he learn to accept fate and whatever the world throws back at him. Faith makes beauty flow from within and turns sadness into laughter, denial into acceptance and sorrow into joy. Faith is a gift from Allah.

Chapter Eleven

"*Khala* Khadeeja, you know I never found good tenants to rent them the ground floor section of my house, and even though I know that my mother already asked you and you declined the offer, I think it's time to give it a second thought. Aisha and I will be more than happy if you took the house," said Hamid one day.

"My son you are very kind and well, I don't know what to say."

I knew I was in no position to decline the offer again. I knew I had to find a way to live after Hassan died. This was no time for stubbornness.

"Say yes, Mama," begged Aisha, and knowing that I had no choice anyway I took the house and we moved right away.

It was a nice house, bigger than the last but with no *housh*. There were three small bedrooms, a kitchen, two bathrooms and a living room. Not having the *housh* made it a bit dull but that was alright I had learned to adjust to everything.

I sold the *dukkan* for a cheap price, much less than I had expected but it was good enough for school fees and a month's necessity. I couldn't possibly allow myself and eight other children to live off Hamid, and my tailoring wasn't doing much, I was already losing my eyesight. If only Mama or Hassan were here they would have had the perfect ideas and I wouldn't have to feel so lonely.

I remembered a friend, a forgotten friend, an old friend of mine who was with me all the way, encouraging me with her looks, giving me hope with her still smile and filling me with optimism with her presence. Layla, my doll Layla, was the only thing I had that didn't abandon me.

"Khadeeja, you forgot who I am," her eyes told me.

"No Layla, you are my soulmate what would I do without you?" I told her.

"You spent all these years giving all you had for others, all your strength and courage even your beauty, dear friend," she seemed to say.

"It's fate, Layla, it's God's fate and I am happy."

"You only think you are, but reality is quite different. I know you miss him."

"He is my life, how can I forget my life?"

"But he forgot you."

"No he didn't, even if he is in the arms of another woman his heart is thinking of me. I know it, I see him in my dreams, I feel him every single day, he smiles when I'm smiling he aches when I cry. My heart tells me he's still there for me and I know he knows I'm still here."

"Live, Khadeeja, and forget the past; you need a man to protect you and your children. Hassan is gone and the boys are young. I am too fragile now, my body is torn and I am growing old. The cloth that covers me is deteriorating and my cotton-stuffed soul is of no use any more."

"We are growing old together and together we will find a good life. No man will ever enter my house. I will protect my family and I will protect you as well as I always have done. You are still the source of my strength and the angel that takes care of me. I love you; I love you more than I ever have before."

Yes I still spoke to her and imagined her answers, though I was an old woman now. I needed to have a friend and she was the only friend I could think of that my heart accepted and trusted. She was the only thing remaining from the past; and my past is what my heart desired. And just as I was whispering into her cloth ears Fatima walked in. "Mama, I need to speak to you."

"What is it baby?"

"You might not like what you hear from me, but Mama, we have to be realistic. Mama, I am the oldest here now. Aisha is happily married and is pregnant. We can't all depend on Hamid. You were able to pay this semester's school fees but what about next semester? What do you have left to sell? Where will we eat from? We are eight and we each have individual needs. Mama, I am in the eleventh grade now but I have decided to quit school and work."

"No, Fatima, God had found us a way every time. He will do the same thing now."

"Mama, you don't understand. If I don't quit school and work I am jeopardizing my sisters' and brothers' educations as well. Please, Mama, I don't think you want to see us all with no education."

In a way I knew she was right, I was jeopardizing their learning, but having her to sacrifice her own education was too much. And where would she work? A young lady working? Unheard of, absurd. Such a scandal might even leave her with no husband. But Fatima insisted and worked so hard to convince me, and knowing that all she was saying was true I soon gave in.

"Where will you work? We have to ask Hamid to look for a job."

"No, Mama, I have already found one. It's in the new beauty salon, you know, the one that just opened by the corner. It's not far from here so I could walk to work as I walked to school."

"And how much will they pay?"

"I will start with five dinars a month. I know it's not much, but at least we can pay for school fees and supplies."

"Go, Fatima. May God be pleased with you as I am and may He grant you a better future for all that you gave up for your family."

"I love you, Mama."

"I love you too.

It was maybe one of the most difficult things I had agreed on but she was right. We were depending on ourselves at least and were proud of it. Fatima was among the first women who worked in Bahrain, and even though the society attacked them fiercely at first they were soon accepted and respected. She worked for many years in the salon and then found a better paid job in the Bahrain international airport. It's so funny, now that I think of it, the big deal I had made when Aisha wanted fashionable dresses for her *jihaz*. I was too worried that Aisha would show her arms and ankles when now the fashion goes even beyond that. It was time for the mini skirts and sleeveless tops and I struggled to keep the girls decently dressed. Bahrain was getting even more influenced with the English rule and everyone agreed that it was time to gain our independence.

★

There was a time I saw my Fatima glowing with joy. Her cheeks were always red, her eyes were always twinkling. She would hum songs of Abdulhalim Hafiz, a famous Egyptian singer who sang love songs, and spread laughter every where she went. Nothing seemed to get on her nerves, not even her whining brothers and sisters, nothing seemed to ruin her mood or bother her. Something was up; I could feel it right there in my heart.

"Fatima, is there something you want to tell me?" I surprised her one day, pretty sure she was up to something.

"Uuummm, maybe," she said shyly.

"Well?"

"There is someone."

"Someone like who?"

"A doctor, he's interested in me."

"And how do you know that?"

"Well, I know him, we have met a couple of times and he wants to meet you. You know, to propose."

"Fatima, my God, all this happened and I am last to know? Where did you meet him? How did you meet him?" I screamed.

"Once when I was working in the salon he was following me to work, and once in the airport he surprised me there, and later I discovered that he'd asked the salon and found out that I was working in the airport. Please, Mama, just meet him and see for yourself."

"You are crazy but what can I say, I will meet him."

Yes she was crazy, and she has always been that way. Fatima was known to do the unexpected and always surprised you with something. Mohammed used to say, "this girl is difficult to raise," and even though he didn't stick around to see it, he was right. And to be honest I was glad she had found a man, that she was in love, for I knew my girl deserved the best.

I met the doctor, Dr. Ali. His family lived in Saudi Arabia but they were Bahrainis.

"We are a big family, nine boys and three girls, half born in Bahrain and the rest in Saudi Arabia," he told me.

"And what do you do now?"

"I still study in England but I am graduating soon, *inshalla*."

"I have heard from Fatima that we are family, we relate in a way?"

"Yes, distant relatives though. Surprisingly we have the same great-great grandfather, so Fatima and I are distant cousins."

That was true actually. Sheikh Ahmed Alkabeer was our great grandfather who left Persia to live in Mecca. Doctor Ali's grandfather stayed in Persia to take care of his father's school and his brother, who was my grandfather, finished his education in another part of Persia far from his hometown. After completing his studies he returned with a family of his own to take care of the school and Ali's grandfather went after his sick father in Mecca and so the two families parted and they never united again.

The engagement was announced soon after but Fatima was so loyal to us she didn't want to have the wedding before making sure each member of the family was taken care of. She worked long hours to ensure enough for their education and needs. She spoiled them in a way, she always had something for them and so they looked forwards to her return from work. The closest to Fatima was Lulwa whom she loved to dress up and take pictures of, and she would spend so much time around them all that they soon started calling her nana, a different form of Mama.

But my Fatima also suffered emotionally. She had to wait for Doctor Ali for a long time, until he was finally done with England and returned to Bahrain. They communicated with letters only and sometimes she didn't receive any which worried her at times and broke her heart at other times. It was difficult to wait for a loved one. No one knew that as much as I did. Sometimes I would hear her cry in her bed and I would sit next to her wanting to soothe her but the words would just disappear and we would both end up crying together. Sometimes she asked for reasons why love had to hurt so much. Sometimes she gave up on his love and pretended not to care but deep inside her she was still waiting for him, for his news, any news. She waited long days, weeks and months until the postman would knock and when he did it was Fatima's *Eid* day.

*

Things were turning around not only for me but also for my Bahrain. I could still remember that day, the day of August 14, 1971. It was probably the most important day in Bahrain's history, for on that day and approximately just before noon all the people, men and women, seniors and children kept close to radio sets, heedless of the summer heat that reached its climax at that time of year. Excitement and anticipation filled the air for everyone believed that the day they were all waiting for had finally arrived. People were on the roads sharing their thrill and waiting impatiently for the big event.

Like everyone else we also waited not knowing what was yet to come. We sat on the rooftop watching, laughing at expressions and imitating the excited. The children didn't understand the importance of that day but I was among those who had waited for long years to live this moment, the moment of turning dreams to reality.

Suddenly the busy street was silent and the voices disappeared in the midsummer humidity.

"From the conference hall at Government House we broadcast a live statement," said the news presenter with a loud and confident voice that echoed across the whole island, and that statement of course was of the independence declaration.

We rejoiced, the people of Bahrain rejoiced. We were free, this island was finally ours and there was no better feeling than freedom. Even the birds were rejoicing, the flowers were smiling and the sun stood proud in the clear blue sky. We were happy; there wasn't a single soul on the island of Bahrain who wasn't happy.

The following day at 11 a.m. the celebration started, marking the end of an era and the start of another. We all clapped as we heard the reporter describing the signing of the document that would put an end to the special agreement which existed between Bahrain and the United Kingdom in the presence of our ruler,

Sheikh Issa bin Salman Al Khalifa on behalf of the leadership and people of Bahrain and Mr. Geoffrey Arthur, who was the political resident and representative of the Queen, on behalf of the British Government.

"Mama what is going on?" asked Noor.

"Well, we are free now. Our country is free," I tried to explain.

"But what does that mean?" she asked curiously.

"I will tell you the story, come with me," shouted Abdul-Jabbar.

"Well, the story started when a man called Mr. Jones, who was in Iran during the time, led a fleet of four warships from the Iranian port to Bahrain. He took over Manama port, and started spreading his army and threatening to use force if Bahrain refrained from signing a treaty with Britain. Sheikh Mohammed, the ruler then, knew that the military force was completely in favor of Britain therefore he decided to sign it though he knew very well that the treaty would give Britain extensive privileges in Bahrain. Since that day the people were praying, hoping that the British existence in the Gulf region in general, and in Bahrain in particular, would come to an end."

"But why the Gulf, why Bahrain?" asked Noor, and I was glad she did for I too was curious.

"Well little girl, let's see what the book says. The British controlled the Gulf because it also wanted to defend its colonies in the Indian sub-continent against potential enemy attacks, so it turned its interests towards the Arabian Gulf in order to form the first defensive line in the passage to its colonies and India. Our Bahrain also had a strategic location, so the British set their eyes on it."

As Abdul-Jabbar finished his story there was another announcement, Bahrain was now officially called the State of Bahrain and the ruler, his highness Sheikh Issa Bin Salman Al Khalifa, was now the Emir of Bahrain.

Yes, it was a good time, a time of peace and tranquility. It was a gift to all of us from our Emir, a gift that would change our lives even more than they were already changing. And it got even better, for Bahrain's independence encouraged the independence of our neighboring states. Only a few weeks' later, on the third of

September of the same year, Qatar declared its independence after signing a friendship agreement with Britain.

*

When all was well and Fatima's fiancé returned, the wedding took place. It was the twelfth of January 1975 and it was a rather unique wedding, one of the biggest in Bahrain. It was the first wedding to be held in a hotel, the Gulf Hotel, for Bahrain was starting to develop after the independence and hotels were among the first new attractions. Doctor Ali brought in flowers from abroad and the chocolates were astonishing. The food was all exotic and the tables were neatly arranged, each with ten chairs and a big flower center piece. It was also very unusual for the groom to see the bride's dress before the wedding but Doctor Ali brought her the wedding dress as well as her *jihaz* from England and it was truly magnificent. The dress had a light pink hue, a breakthrough from the typical white one. It didn't have a veil but instead a beautiful classical hat that matched the dress. It had beige embroidered flowers and a train that moved swiftly behind her. She was beautiful, she was a queen and I could tell that Doctor Ali loved the way she looked that night.

Doctor Ali then worked in a new local hospital. They took a small house not far away from ours and Aisha's and as I expected, Fatima was soon pregnant. They were happy and I was happy. She deserved a good life after all her sacrifices and I needed to see my daughter happy, to know that God had finally rewarded her for such a good, passionate heart. Two gone, and seven looking ahead to a hopefully brighter future.

Chapter Twelve

"I heard my second daughter got married," whispered Mohammed to the moon.

He had grown so old and weak, and to him life was worth nothing. He was lost but that was how he felt since he left the first time.

"Why didn't you tell me she was getting married? How did my love take care of the expenses now that Brother Hassan is dead?"

There were times he would scream at the moon as if it was to blame for all he went through.

"What are you doing, old man, sitting by the window like that? Don't tell me you're waiting for a princess or an angel to appear," his wife screamed sarcastically.

"Leave me alone, woman," he screamed back.

He knew Khadeeja would never speak to him that way; he knew she would never hurt him or disrespect him. He wondered where she was, what she was doing, what she looked like, and he cried.

"How pathetic, a man your age crying, now tell me, what are you crying for?"

"I said leave me alone woman, go visit your friends or something, what are you doing here?"

"I am going but Mustafa Agha invited you as well. Now don't tell me you're not coming, you know how important this man is and you will embarrass the family if you don't come."

"I am not going."

"Mohammed, I said—"

"Shut up, woman, can't you leave me for once."

He was tired of her. He was tired of her attitude and her constant nagging. He was tired of being pushed around like a small child.

She did not give up, she knew that someone like Mustapha Agha could finance a business she was thinking of and someone like Mohammed could ruin this chance for her. She had been working on her relationship with Zakia, his wife, so she could reach her goal, for she had been dreaming about it forever and now she wouldn't allow him to ruin it.

"A showroom, a big showroom surrounded with rows and rows of textiles. Persian silk and Indian chiffon, Egyptian cotton and Turkish velvet. Dyed material with the brightest colors any eye has ever seen, plain and flowery, soft and rough, all kinds, everything any woman has ever dreamed of," she whispered to herself. "No, Mohammed, I will not let you ruin my dream, not now, not when I am so very close to it."

She marched up and down trying to think of a way. It was the evening prayer and Mohammed was getting ready to pray. She looked at him in despise and ran to her neighbors' house as quick as she could so she would be able to return before he even noticed her disappearance. Of course she knew Mohammed didn't care, but when the house suddenly became quiet then he would assume she was gone somewhere.

"Khanom, is your husband here?" she asked the neighbor's wife.

"Yes, he is. Are you alright?"

"Just imagine, Mohammed doesn't want to go to Mustafa Agha's party tonight."

"But he must, no one can say no to Mustafa Agha, no one at all."

"Please speak to your husband, let him convince Mohammed, I can't possibly go, ashamed this way, knowing my husband is a disgrace."

"Don't worry, I will tell him. You go get ready now or you'll be late."

She ran back to the house and saw Mohammed where she had left him, still praying and crying as usual. She hated that scene, the scene of a weak man. She knew there was nothing that bonded them; his heart was somewhere else and she didn't care. She knew she was not beautiful, not sexy, or even attractive. All she had was money and only little was left of it now. But he wouldn't leave her, that much she knew. He couldn't go back after all these years to his old life, no one would accept him, no one would approve.

He would stay as he was, pathetic and holding on to the past with no hope or faith.

There had been a time when she was in love with him. She was in love with his masculine nature, his handsome face and muscular body. His charm was breathtaking and his strong personality was spectacular.

He worked for her father for some time, as a trader, that was. He had nothing at first but he soon gained the father's trust and was promised more if he would marry the daughter. He was desperate for money, for a new life, and so the marriage was to be the only way out and a new start.

Though she loved him she knew she would never win him, for his heart was holding on to the past. Her jealousy soon turned to anger and she took over her father's trade simply to provoke him but he didn't care. He kept on wondering and kept his distance from her, wishing it had all been a bad dream. They went out of business just a year after her father's death and Mohammed was in a neverending state of depression.

The door knocked and she realized she was already late for an important evening.

"Good evening, is Mohammed home?" said the neighbor.

"Please do come in, he is inside, I really hope you can convince him," she said.

Even the neighbor despised her. It was impolite for a woman to interfere in her husband's matters and it was even worse to involve people but he had to obey for no one rested from her filthy tongue.

He followed her inside a small room where he saw Mohammed still praying. Throughout these years that they had been neighbors he had wondered about Mohammed's secret. Why was he living such a life? What was killing him slowly and why did he refuse to live with inner peace? He looked fragile, weak and sad, and only got worse with time. He was such a respectful, noble man, what did this woman do to him to make him so ashamed of himself?

"Hello my dear brother, I apologize for keeping you waiting but I didn't know you were coming and…"

"No, no, your home is my home and my home is yours, I didn't mind waiting at all."

"May Allah bless you."

"Brother Mohammed, I have a favor to ask you and I hope you can help me with it."

"If it's something I can handle be sure I will not put you down."

"You know about Mustafa Agha's party tonight? It's just that I hate those parties and I was hoping that, if we went together, then it wouldn't be too bad."

"But I wasn't planning to go."

"Brother Mohammed, you know how this society is, we have to go, both of us."

"Times are changing. We don't have to do anything any more. This society will be against you anyway."

"As you please, Brother Mohammed, I will see you soon."

The neighbor stood up to leave and Mohammed couldn't let him go broken-hearted like that. He walked towards him and gave him a promise, "I will come on one condition," he said.

"Please, anything."

"We don't stay more than half an hour."

The neighbor hugged him gratefully and left contentedly.

She was standing outside all dressed up and waiting impatiently for the result, and seeing a smile on the man's face gave her the answer. She rushed inside to find Mohammed in his *thoub* looking angrier than ever. He knew she was behind it and she saw it clearly. She was pleased with herself and he only hated her more.

"You will never be like her," he whispered to himself.

She was all dressed up from head to toe but she was nothing compared to Khadeeja. He remembered her in her blue turquoise *thoub* and elegant jewelry. Her neatly braided hair was decorated with *mashmoum*. She was something; she was one of a kind.

He forced himself to go with his neighbor and counted the seconds until he could leave. He knew his wife was going to speak to Mustafa about business and he didn't want to stay for more insults from her. He was ashamed of what was on her mind.

"The night is young, Mohammed, where are you going?" said Mustafa.

"Well I can't stay up late, I am tired. Please excuse me?"

"You're young, Mohammed, live a little, enjoy, life is short after all."

"Please sir, it was an honor to spend an evening with you and I am sure you and your guests will enjoy the rest of the night, but as for me, I have to call it a night."

They shook hands and went in opposite directions, one to his party and the other to his dreams.

As soon as he walked in Mohammed rushed to the window and took his usual seat. He looked up searching for his new best friend, the moon; maybe it carried news about his Khadeeja.

★

Mariam and Dana graduated from high school the following year and worked, and a year after Abdurrahman went to Kuwait to finish his studies. Abdul-Jabbar was content with his high school diploma and worked right away.

There is nothing like watching your children succeed in their lives. They matured so quickly I could hardly catch up. The girls were beautiful and the boys made me proud. Every time I looked into their eyes I couldn't help think how much Mohammed was missing and how good a job I had done raising them this way.

"Do you see them Layla, do you see these beings I have brought to this world? Do you see how amazing they grew to be?" I whispered into Layla's cloth ear.

"Yes dear friend, they are truly angels," I heard her say.

"Do you think Mohammed would have been proud if he was here?"

"Of course he would, look at them, who wouldn't be?"

"He's missing so much."

"Yes he is, but please stop thinking about him and live your life, Khadeeja, for once enjoy it. Give all the credit to yourself… It's your hard work not any one else's," said her sad eyes.

"Yes, I know, but they have my Mohammed's blood running through their veins, he has to share them with me, he has to… He has to see his pride and joy."

"But he's not here, and God knows if he'll ever be here."

"I know he's not here, Layla, but I also know that my heart is telling him every single day."

The house was quieter now, more than it had ever been. I missed Mama, I missed Hassan and to my surprise I missed Mohammed even more. I wished I knew where he was, not to go after him but just for the sake of it. I wanted to know if he was happy, if he had kids, and mostly if he had totally forgotten about us. Abdul-Jabbar reminded me of his father. He had his looks, his personality, and his style, whereas Abdurrahman was more like Hassan.

Aunty Jameela, the only aunty I had, moved to Kuwait and died a month later. She suffered from cancer and refused any kind of treatment whatsoever until she died four months after. Aziz came back to Bahrain but we never saw each other. I never tried to contact him and he didn't even ask about us. He divorced his wife a long time ago and never got to trust women again. Deep inside me I was hoping he would stop by one day, but he never did as I had expected in the first place. The things I was hearing about him made me ashamed anyway.

"Baba won't stop marrying and divorcing women. There's always someone new in his life," Abdullah told me, "it's very embarrassing but he won't listen to any of us. He married nine women after Mama and not one of them stayed more than a year."

Aisha had three children and Fatima had one. What a beautiful thing to see your grandchild, more beautiful than seeing your own child. I would wait impatiently for Friday when they would come to have lunch with me and my family would be reunited again and when they left the house almost feels haunted.

*

It was late one night and I was sitting with Abdurrahman in his room. We were in the middle of a discussion when we heard a knock on the house door. Who would visit us at such a time? My first thoughts were Aisha and Fatima. Was something wrong? But now that Abdurrahman got us a telephone they would definitely call and not drop in this way. Could it be him? Had he finally come back? Abdurrahman went to open the door and I rushed after him.

"Who is it?"

"We are Khadeeja's relatives, open the door now," they seemed to whisper.

"Well, it's late, she is asleep," said Abdurrahman, crossly.

"Wake her, it's important."

"My mother has no relatives."

"We come from her father's side and it's not nice to question guests at the door like this."

"And not nice to visit people at such a time."

I pushed him aside and opened the door. There were two women and a man. The women instantly barged into the house as the man preferred to wait outside. Could my father have such rude members in his family?

"So you are Khadeeja," said one.

"May I help you?"

"Aren't you going to invite us in?"

I took them to the living room though I really felt like throwing them out. They each took off their *abaya* revealing their big bodies and old fashioned but expensive silk dresses. Their curly hair fell loosely on their shoulders and their round faces had no beauty. After all these years what could they possibly want? And why hadn't Mama mentioned them to me?

"Khadeeja, we are here as your family. You carry our name, our surname, so to people we are family."

"I am happy to meet you, I never knew any of my father's family. How do we exactly relate?"

"I am Saidah, Abdullah's sister, and this is Nadia, our younger sister."

My eyes filled with tears from happiness. My aunts, my very own aunts came looking for me, for their niece. All of a sudden their ugliness disappeared. I wanted to hug them; I couldn't wait to hug them. I stood up and walked towards my Aunt Saidah and reached for her hand but she removed them and turned away.

"Khadeeja, this is no time for emotions and all that crap. We are here to say one thing and leave; you will never see us again," said Nadia.

"I am so happy to see you. I don't understand why all the anger and hostility."

"We are ashamed of you, it's simply that."

"Excuse me?"

"We are a famous family, everyone knows us. We are known for our power and money, and the idea that one of us lives the way you do is a disgrace."

I was so shocked with what I had heard that I felt paralyzed. I couldn't think of anything, I could not say anything. I sat there, a dummy taking their insults one by one like arrows across my heart.

"We will give you money, we will make you rich, a better house, better schools, and we will leave, we will disappear and you will never hear from us again."

"Please leave my house at once."

"What? Nadia, please listen to this, a beggar and we offer her a whole new life and she wants to throw us out."

"Leave now!"

"Listen, dear, we are not doing this out of love or honor. We are doing this for our family's name."

"For a second, for only one second I felt I was the happiest. I thought, finally I met my father's family. Finally I could imagine him and see where he really came from. But now you are nothing, you are a nightmare. Leave my house. You don't have to save your name or lose any money on me. This name does not exist to me. From this day onwards I do not belong to this family. Leave now."

They each looked at each other and grabbed their *abaya*s. They looked at me and ran out the door in anger.

"You will be sorry for this," said Saidah, as I slammed the door in her face.

I ran into my room and threw myself on the bed. Mama loved Baba so much, he couldn't possibly be one of them. Mama was protecting me all this time that must be why she never talked about them. I wondered what she really thought about them. I wondered if my father was proud of them. I wondered if they ever liked my mother, for it seemed very unlikely. What a funny world. When you really want something and finally find it you realize you never wanted it or needed it in the first place. All my life I wanted to know where I really came from. Where were my relatives and what were they like? On that day I realized that a person's identity is not in the surname or relatives or a certain place. It's who you really are, your heart, your soul, your beliefs and goals. On that day I was proud of myself like never before. Now I didn't have to wonder about my father's family any more. Now they were history and already a forgotten history. I decided that I would never mention this to anyone or even allow myself to think about it ever again. I called Abdurrahman who was anxiously waiting outside my room and decided not to tell him either. It was the best way to forget.

"Who were they, Mother?"

"Just people... Weird people as you can clearly see," I said as I laughed, trying hard to ease the moment.

"Are you alright?"

"Yes I am. They come from Iran and they wanted to drop by, see if I wanted anything from them... They are leaving soon."

"Oh, I see. But they were very rude. I think you are hiding something, Mama. With all due respect, I think you are lying."

"Maybe I am... But let's just call it a small lie. It's nothing really son, it's really nothing. Let's have some tea now, shall we?"

And with that we never mentioned that incident ever again. It was truly a forgotten history though a very wounding one.

★

Mariam soon got married to one of our neighbors, Yousif, just as I had expected. They had clicked from the first time they met and I knew Fatima khalo, Yousif's mother, had her eyes set on Mariam since she was a child. The wedding was small, everything happened in one day and they stayed in a rented apartment not very far from us.

Yousif was a good man. He had a remarkable sense of humor and an intelligent mind. They met by coincidence when I was making a dress for his mother and he came to pick it up. Mariam opened the door and with the first look the two of them were hooked with love. Yousif proposed many times but I was waiting for Fatima khalo who was living in Kuwait until her husband's sudden death. A month after she had settled in Bahrain she came to visit me with Yousif and I knew it was the day I would give my daughter away.

Mariam sat next to her future mother-in-law, both with confidence and trying to make a good impression at the same time. She constantly laughed in shyness and he tried to start any kind of conversation with her. She sat like a royal, talked like one and acted like one. She was happy.

Fatima khalo too was happy. She was proud of her son's choice and insisted that the wedding take place right away. I was glad to see her impressed with Mariam's hard work and I was glad that my daughter would be part of a good family.

Dana was the one who killed me the most. She was a hard worker but radical too. She loved her freedom and liberty and had a very strong personality, very different than her quiet self when she was much younger. She wanted much more than what she had, and her ambition and enthusiasm always got her what she wanted. Even when her father left, she had chosen to look forwards rather to than think of the loss like the rest of us; "Baba wanted another life and so he went to look for it. I also want a better life and will prove to Baba some day that we were better off without him anyway," she told me once. And maybe she was right; maybe we were better off without him.

"Why are we still living here?" she asked me once, "we should look for a better place, we can afford it."

"But Lulwa, Noor, and Layla are still in school and in no time they will be going to college. I don't think we can afford renting something now."

"Why not? Abdurrahman has come back from Kuwait and he found a wonderful job, Abdul-Jabbar just got promoted, and I am doing fine as well. What can't we afford?"

"Well, college fees are getting more expensive every year, not to forget the books and all that stuff. No baby, really, we are fine the way we are."

"No you are not." Doctor Ali and Fatima walked in.

"We have a surprise for all of you," screamed Fatima.

"Well, what is it?"

"Ali bought a big plot of land, a very big plot of land, in Sanad village. It's kind of far from here but it's a beautiful area. We are surrounded with palm trees and are closer to the sea, away from this growing city," said Fatima.

"Wow, that is great," said Dana.

"No, you didn't hear the great part yet," jumped in Fatima, "go ahead Ali, you tell them."

"What is it, my son?" I was already filled with curiosity and my heart skipped beats.

"Well, Fatima and I decided that the land is too big for us so we decided to share it," explained Doctor Ali.

"That is a good idea. You know you could rent it to someone or sell part of it for a higher price, or keep it as an investment," said Dana, interestedly.

"We could do that or we could do something much better," Doctor Ali answered. "We could give half of it to *Khala* Khadeeja and she can do with it as she pleases."

I couldn't believe my ears. I never owned a piece of land. As a matter of fact, it had been a while since I owned anything. But what would I do with this land? How would it be useful to me and my children? Too many things rushed into my head all at once, so many that I even forgot the most important one, if I should accept such a thing.

"My son, that is so kind, but what would an old woman like me do with the land?" I asked.

"*Khala* Khadeeja there is much you could do. Why don't you sit down and talk with Abdurrahman, Abdul-Jabbar and Dana. They are experienced in investments now, they will probably come up with the best idea."

And so Doctor Ali left us to discuss the land issue, not accepting any kind of refusal, and Fatima was jumping with joy and proud of her husband at the same time. She should be, for he was truly a good man.

★

Sickness was taking over Mohammed slowly and grief was his new best friend. Time was really punishing him for what he had done, as if guilt alone wasn't enough.

He felt Nader's poisoned blood was now in his body, spreading little by little. He no longer made use of his legs and the wheelchair was his companion. It was only a matter of time before he would not be able to use his hands and he knew that. His wife, his rich wife, paid him no attention any more. His eldest daughter was getting married but to a man he knew nothing about. They didn't even ask for his blessing; Amina found a good match, a relative, and went ahead with the arrangements.

"You are in no position for people to see you like this, in a chair. I would rather you not attend the wedding, you will only embarrass your daughter," she told him.

They were slowly losing the money Amina had inherited, and with Mohammed unable to work a lot of changes had to be made. The mansion was no longer their mansion, they moved to a different neighborhood, and the few people who remained Mohammed's friends weren't allowed to find him for the area, the house and everything in it was a disgrace to Amina. And she was angry, angry at everything; her husband, her children, the society, everything, but only one paid for it, only Mohammed.

He wanted to run away, to a place where no one knew him, an unknown place. He wanted to leave this life with all its evil vibes and forget about all the humiliation he was causing them, but it was too late, he knew it was too late. It was only his son, Faisal, who showed some concern. It was he who fed him, bathed him, changed him and helped him if he needed anything, but Faisal was also a student, he couldn't be a full-time nurse to his father, and Amina did all that she could to keep her son away from the mortifying father. He had lost it all; his dignity, his pride, his health, his life, he lost it all. When did it all happen? When did he ruin his life? The day he took the ship to Dubai, and he knew that.

*

It was a sunny day, December 16, 1979. The neighborhood was jammed with people for it was the national day carnival. Zainabi, a neighbor famous for her homemade sweets, had set up a booth in the corner selling sweets. Farkhunda was just opposite making her famous falazing, special kind of bread. Jassim and his younger brother had a puppet show for the children and there was also the laywa, a special dance, preformed by the Bahraini national band all over the place.

It was one of these days that we all waited for. We enjoyed watching all the people in their best from the rooftop. We would take some tea and nuts, biscuits and halwa (a Bahraini sweet). It's like a customary picnic, something we used to do with Mohammed every year and continued to do so after he left. Even Aisha and her children would join us. It was wonderful, we loved our small island and we loved celebrating its independence.

Abdul-jabbar took one of Aisha's children to buy some more sweets from Zainabi and we watched them dance with the crowd on their way.

I watched with pride until I saw them standing with a stranger, a young boy, rather handsome. They walked side-by-side and I thought they must be friends or something, but Abdul-Jabbar had a weird expression on his face. They stood for a moment by the house door. I watched them very closely with an uncertain feeling. It was like I knew the boy, there was something about him.

They walked in and my heart started beating so fast. No male strangers were ever allowed into our home and I couldn't understand why Abdul-Jabbar would invite him in when he knew the rules. In no time they were standing in front of me. Abdul-Jabbar's face was stiff and the boy was shy. He couldn't even look at us and his thin, fragile hands were shivering.

"Mama, Mama, this is Faisal, Uncle Abdul-Jabbar says he is my uncle," cried Aisha's child.

Upon hearing these words I felt my whole body suddenly numb. Tears filled my eyes and butterflies filled my stomach. I couldn't believe that Mohammed's son was standing there next to his brother but a strange man to me.

"Welcome to your home, son. Why don't you come join your brothers and sisters and enjoy our carnival? Make room, girls." I forced myself to speak.

Faisal was Mohammed's only son from his second marriage. He looked so much like his brother, Abdurrahman. He was thin, not very healthy looking. There was something about him that was wrong. I watched him very closely and he tried so hard to make a good impression. The children looked nervous and uncomfortable. They didn't know how to react; his visit was a surprise and I could see how curious they all looked.

"This is a beautiful day, *Khala* Khadeeja, I am glad you invited me to stay," he said in a surprised tone. He didn't expect me to welcome him, I could clearly tell.

"You can come anytime, my son, your brothers' house is your house."

"I wonder if I can have a word with you in private, if you don't mind?"

"If you have something to say to her then say it here. I don't see why you should speak to her in private," said Abdurrahman, in hostility. He was trying to protect me but I didn't need any protection, particularly from this fragile boy.

"Don't you dare raise your voice in my presence again, specially towards your brother. Son, please follow me. The rest of you try to give us some privacy and don't you dare interfere."

I took Faisal into the bedroom and closed the door behind him.

"Aisha, could you fix us some tea, please," I called out.

"Mama, what are you doing?" whispered Aisha.

"The boy wants to talk, damn it, we should listen to him. He is your brother, Aisha, and this is real. He is here and I will find out the purpose of his coming."

I went back into the bedroom filled with curiosity and fear. What made him come here, what did he want from me? Had something happened to Mohammed?

I sat down next to him. He looked sad, I felt like hugging him. I looked into his eyes and saw them searching for love, searching for compassion. He was lost, he was scared and I made him nervous.

"Well, what is it, son?" I said.

"*Khala* Khadeeja, I came to apologize on behalf of my father for all that you went through."

His words shocked me even more. Did Mohammed send this young boy to apologize? Does Mohammed even remember us after all this time?

"Did he ask you to apologize?" I asked.

"No *Khala*, I came on my own."

"But it's not your fault."

"I know it isn't, but *Khala* Khadeeja I am dying. I had to see you and my brothers and sisters. I felt that I had to apologize no matter what I had to make sure you were alright. After all you are also my family."

"You are dying?" I asked.

"I have leukemia, *Khala* Khadeeja, I am dying."

I looked at this poor boy and cried. I cried because I already loved him. I loved him because I saw Mohammed's weakness in him. He was part of my Mohammed and so he was part of me. He was too beautiful to die. Was God punishing Mohammed?

"Leukemia?" I managed to say… I didn't know what else to say.

"*Khala* Khadeeja, I knew I had a family, I knew you existed and I knew you were the most wonderful family. The Prophet, peace be upon him, always talked about family, how we should take care of each other and love one another."

"God bless you, child, but how did you know we even existed?"

"My father has been in seclusion for many years and I didn't know what was wrong or how I could help him. Until one night I surprised him in his room where he sat for long hours by the window, staring at the moon and sometimes even talking to it. I walked towards him and saw him crying, 'Please forgive me, I beg for your forgiveness. Please take care of my family in Bahrain, for they have no one, I beg you, Lord,' he whispered without noticing I was there with him.

"'Who are they? Your family in Bahrain? What have you done to feel so guilty all these years?' I asked. He turned to me in surprise trying to wipe his tears, trying to hide them.

"'Go away, what are you doing here?' he screamed. But I couldn't go away. I couldn't leave him like this.

"'Baba, why are you pushing me away, I am your only son Baba, and I want to...' Before I even could finish my sentence he screamed back at me.

"'No you're not, you are not my only son.' He fell to the floor and cried like a baby. Though I was shocked I couldn't help holding him and rocking him like a baby. It was only then that I first felt his love and passion. He was in pain all these years and none of us knew anything about it. He told me the whole story, *Khala* Khadeeja, he cried and I cried. He talked so much about you and I fell in love with you, your family. He loved you all so much and his words made me love you too.

"A couple of months later I found out I had leukemia. I decided to come to Bahrain. I knew I had little time but I needed to make the best of the time I had and this was my first decision. Baba tried to stop me, not because he didn't want me to see you but because he was afraid of the reaction. Mama of course thinks I am on a trip with my friends; there was no need to tell her."

"You have Mohammed's wisdom," I told him.

"And you have my father's heart," he replied.

I couldn't believe Faisal said that to me. He gave me hope all over again. He gave me more love than I had ever had. I embraced him, I embraced him so hard, not as Mohammed's child but as my own. He loved us without knowing us, he loved us through Mohammed's words, through his guilt, and now he was dying. Why was life so difficult?

As we left the room I could see them all staring questioningly. I held him close to me and could already see the looks on their faces.

"Faisal will be staying with us for a couple of days," I said.

"Here in this house?" asked Lulwa.

"Well, isn't he your brother? This is his home," I insisted.

My children were never unwelcoming but they didn't know what to do. It was an unusual situation and it all needed some time until they get used to the whole idea.

And I was right.

The following day they were all surrounding Faisal, giving him all the love and attention he needed. He was happy; the poor boy laughed at times and told stories at other times. The children loved hearing his stories about their father and sisters. They wanted to learn more about Dubai and how people lived there. And I loved to see them together. Faisal was able to win them as he won me, and it was beautiful. I wished Mohammed was here to see it, I wished he could see all the love that was in my home.

There was no room for hatred, there was no room for jealousy in my house and Faisal saw that. I could see he was happy here with us and we all hoped it would last forever, but we all knew he had to leave. The day had come for his return.

It was a sad day. Tears filled our eyes as we said goodbye. We all knew it would be the last time; though we prayed for his health and a long life, we could see that sickness was all over his face. It was a rather sad day.

I watched Abdul-Jabbar and Abdurrahman walk him to the port, both trying to hide their tears. Faisal though looked peaceful. He was not only bidding his family farewell, he was saying it to the whole world.

"May God protect you, my son," I whispered as they disappeared.

★

The kids were busy discussing the best choices about Dr. Ali's proposal as I fixed them dinner. The younger ones joined in too and their seriousness soon transformed this into a hilarious gathering.

"I know," jumped Dana.

"What?" everyone screamed from all directions.

"We will use it ourselves, we will build a house."

"Build a house what are you talking about?" asked Abdurrahman.

"You are dreaming again, aren't you?" said Abdul-Jabbar sarcastically.

"Dana, don't put ideas in your head that are too good to be true." I said.

"Would you please all listen before you attack?" shouted Dana, defending herself,

"Abdurrahman, Abdul-Jabbar, and I all have really good jobs. We could get a loan from a bank and build ourselves a house, our home, Mama's home. We can't live in this place forever, and besides, Aisha's family is growing and one floor isn't enough. We have land that we could use and we could all share the loan payment."

"That does make sense in a way," said Abdurrahman.

"I don't know. These things take forever, and don't forget the interest rates. It's not as easy as it sounds."

But the discussion went on, followed by research, and Doctor Ali joined in the plan and in no time the base was set.

★

The house took nearly a year to be completed and it was definitely a dream house. It wasn't very big but not small either, with three bedrooms, two bathrooms, two living rooms, a big aluminum kitchen and a storage room. It had all the luxuries I dreamt of, an electric oven, dishwasher, washing machine and dryer, air conditioning in every room, all that you can think of. Fatima's house, which was built much earlier than our house, stood in the opposite direction and both houses were surrounded with a beautiful garden and a swimming pool.

But just as I thought that things were finally taking on a good course the unexpected happened.

"Mama, I am getting married," Dana surprised me.

What did she mean by 'I am getting married'? What kind of marriage is that? I was hurt. I was stabbed in the heart by my own daughter who didn't respect me as her mother and ask me if she could marry; rather she told me, only gave me the news as if she was telling me she was off to work or to one of her sisters' houses.

"Getting married? And is this a way for girls to get married these days?"

"I know you won't approve."

"And why wouldn't I?"

"Because he is a Christian British man."

This girl was out of her mind. I was so angry that I wanted to slap her but I tried to control myself and pray for patience until I could make sense of her crap.

"You know I won't approve but you want to go ahead and do it anyway. What a disgrace."

"Why would it be a disgrace? We work together and we fell in love, what is wrong in that?'

"He is a Christian. Would you explain to me how a Muslim girl can marry a Christian. Do you want to be an outlaw to your own religion?"

"He will convert so we can get married."

"And you think you will be happy?"

"Of course, I love him and he loves me."

"And you think that love is enough? Well, you are wrong. Look at your mother's life, and you saw how Baba and I were in love."

"Mama, I am getting married and that's that."

The whole family was angry at the idea of Dana's marriage but she fought for herself and her loved one. Her brothers were so angry at her that they stopped talking to her, and so were her older sisters. The younger ones though were very understanding of her situation, which made me even more worried. Was this an outrageous generation? How on earth am I supposed to protect them from such terrible things from happening? I was deep in thought when I heard loud screams, shouting, crying, and banging. I could feel my body shivering as I ran, I could hardly breathe when I saw Lulwa, Noor, and Looloo trembling and crying fearfully in the corner of the room as Abdul-Jabbar, Abdurrahman, Aisha, Mariam, and Fatima all screamed at dejected Dana. At that moment I felt like holding her close to me, in my arms like the day I brought her into this world. I wanted to protect her as any mother would protect her child. But I stood there knowing that this time I could not do anything. Dana was going towards the wrong direction, she was going against her religion, her family, her traditions; and her brothers and sisters couldn't watch her do such a thing without interfering.

But she looked sad; she was fighting for her love with all she had. Her eyes ached for support which her heart knew was impossible. Her thin hands were quivering; she was holding back the tears. And even though I was right there in front of her, I felt I was miles away.

"Mama, only you can understand how I feel," she surprised me.

"Are you willing to give up your family for love?" I asked, trying so hard to hide my affection.

"Weren't you willing to give up everything for Baba?"

"Not my religion, not my family."

"Don't you want to see me happy?"

"How do you know that your happiness is with this man?"

"He loves me, he respects me, and he is everything I ever wanted."

"And how are you going to live away from your family? What are we supposed to tell people?" shouted Fatima.

"I am the one getting married, not the people... Besides if Mama survived after Baba left her I am sure I can as well."

"Don't you dare compare yourself with Mama... Or..." screamed Abdurrahman until I stopped them all with a cry even I was surprised with.

I could not handle it any more. Watching my own family break up like that. My arms were always their true home but now my arms were not enough any more. I went into my room, locked the door and fell to my knees into prayer. It was obvious I could not stop Dana or change her mind, and the family would never forgive her. It will never be the same again... ever.

I could still remember her first smile, first laugh, first word and first footsteps. She was always ahead of them all, the clever one.

"This one is going to be out of control," I remember Mohammed saying once, "she's going to be just like her daddy," as he laughed.

What was he to say about this matter? Would he give in to his daughter's love or would he do the impossible to stop it? Would he bless her or would he throw her out?

I was lost, I cried all night as I prayed for a miracle. My family was all I had and to watch it break up the way it was killed me. I knew this was a test from God so I had to be strong but I just didn't know what it was I should do. I prayed and prayed until I fell asleep on the *sujadhh* in a faint. I felt nothing until Lulwa woke me up for the *fajr* prayers.

God has special ways of dealing with things. I woke up with a confident soul and the strength to face this obstacle. I was sad but I just knew Allah would take care of it all and all I had to do was sit back and watch him work.

The morning sun soon announced the beginning of another day, but this day was special. I knew that this day was going to be full of surprises. Good or bad, I didn't know, but something was bound to happen. The girls went to school and Dana rushed out without even a morning kiss or her usual glass of fresh orange juice. Her eyes were swollen and I knew she had been crying all night. My heart grieved for my daughter but I tried to stay strong as much as I could.

I tried to keep my distance from everyone all day long. I could see how they all watched me closely, waiting for a comment, for an action, for a tear; anything that would tell them how I was thinking. But I kept my distant hoping that the day would pass in peace.

It was past eight in the evening and I was worried about Dana, she rarely was late and under such circumstances I simply knew it wasn't a good sign.

The moon started to lose its shine, the palm trees looked strange, the wind stopped blowing and there was no sign of Dana.

The girls went to sleep, the boys ignored the matter and I was troubled.

I marched up and down the room and wandered in the dark garden, hoping, praying for her safety and return.

As I stepped into my room to grab the Quran, desperate for comfort, I heard the door and I knew it must be her. In less than a second I found her in front of me. I walked towards her wanting to hold her but her words slapped me so strongly I felt my heavy body losing its balance and falling from distress.

"James converted and I am leaving tonight," she said angrily and walked out of the house with all her bags, not leaving a trace.

Another shock and another sad day to add to my depressing memory but grief was my companion and I had to face it.

The house was never the same again. Dana's memories were in every corner and though she was alive and happy somewhere in the world, to me she was dead. I missed her, I missed her since day one and I lived the pain of losing my mama, Nader, Mohammed, and Hassan all over again. I was worried about the young ones, I was worried about their present and future. My family was going to suffer; society could attack us as it had so many times before. But I knew deep inside me that God wanted it this way so it must be good, there must be a good side to it all and therefore I should be content.

"*Khala* Khadeeja, I am Sumaya, Dana's friend from work." A young girl surprised me a couple of days later.

"Please do come in. I didn't know she had a friend called Sumaya."

"Well, I only met her recently. *Khala* I can't come in, I have to go back to work. I have something for you; it's a letter from Dana. She asked me to give it to you in person."

I took the letter with a hurry, eager to know its contents, but it wasn't appropriate to have this stranger read something so personal. I hid it in my pocket as if in fear of losing it, unable to hide my happiness and fear at the same time.

"Thank you, I apologize for troubling you."

"Not at all. Please do excuse me, I have to go now."

I watched her leave and I ran into the house like a horse that had just been set free.

"Looloo, where are you? Just when you need them these children disappear like ghosts in the dark."

"I am here, I am here, I was reading."

"Come into my room at once."

"Mama, I swear I didn't use your powder, it must be Noor or Lulwa. I didn't do it, I swear."

"What powder, you silly girl? I have something important but you have to swear you won't tell anyone. It will be our secret. Do you promise?"

"Yes I do, Mama, tell me, what is going on?"

"Have you ever heard about a girl called Sumaya?"

"Maybe you should talk to Lulwa then."

"Why, is there something I should know?"

"Well, Sumaya is behind it all. Lulwa knows her better."

"Okay, go call Lulwa, but don't mention what I had just asked you… no one, you hear me?"

"Yes, Mama, I promise."

There was much more to the story than I knew. Lulwa walked in trembling. I should have known before. I should have known the girls knew something. They were hiding something.

"Sit down, Lulwa."

"I m sorry I know I should have told you before you found out by yourself."

"You didn't think Sumaya would come all the way here, did you?"

"No. How dare she?"

"What makes you say that?"

"Sumaya was behind Dana's marriage. She introduced them to each other and always invited them out together. She was behind it."

"No one is behind anything. She might have made it easier for them to get to know each other but she definitely is not to blame."

"Then who is, Mama? Who is to blame for breaking up our family this way? Our sister will never come back again ever," cried Lulwa bitterly.

"Fate. Blame fate. Lulwa, you are a woman of faith. You are a strong believer. You must understand that it's the way God wanted it to be. We have to keep our faith in Him."

"But my sister…"

"Your sister will come back someday. There is too much anger now. Maybe it's better that way. Who knows what would have happened if she had stayed? It's only a matter of time. I need time, she needs time, and the whole family needs time. It's only a matter of time."

"I hope she returns one day. But Mama you didn't tell me, what did Sumaya want?"

"Now, you must not tell anyone what I am about to share with you."

"I won't, Mama, I won't."

"Sumaya brought in a letter from Dana. I want you to read it."

I gave the letter to Lulwa and we were both excited and scared. She sat down on the floor beside me and in a whisper started to read the letter.

Dear Mama,

I am sad that it had to end this way. Of all the people, I truly believed that you would be the one who would understand me the most. I truly believed that you would stand by me to protect me, your daughter.

Mama, you know love. You were once in love and until this day you stood in the face of the whole society, in the face of whoever stood against you, to protect your love. Was it your choice? Did you choose to love him and then wait for him for the rest of your life after he left you? Did you choose to be hurt and confused?

Like you, Mama, I did not choose when or where or how or who to love. It chose me. Like you, I couldn't let go easily now that I've found love. He was the only man, the only man I ever loved or will love for many many years to come.

By the time you receive my letter I will be gone. I will be a wife, his wife, and I will be miles away from you, from the only home I knew, to start my own home, my own family with the man of my dreams, the man I love and the man who loves me. Love knows no age, no race or religion. Love is pure of these materialistic values only society has enforced upon us. I will be in England with my husband and my home, your arms, your love and constant prayers will remain a beautiful memory.

I know you will think of me as I will think of you but I pray that they be happy thoughts, far away from anger and hatred. I love you. I have always loved you.

Forgive me if I have wronged you but someday, someday you will understand why I went away. You will understand why I stood up for my love. I know you will understand, you among all others, because you lived a love story, the most beautiful love story I have ever heard of.

Pray for me. Forgive me.
Truly yours,
Dana

Lulwa and I held each other and cried. Maybe because we already understood her. Maybe because we regretted letting her go. I wished I had given her a last hug. I wished for so many things. It is difficult to lose a child, your child, probably the most difficult thing in the world. And now I have lost one, another one.

Chapter Thirteen

Things were pretty slow after that. Abdurrahman got married and left to work in Jeddah, Saudi Arabia, and Abdul-Jabbar, who also married, his cousin, Fatin, was planning to follow his uncle's and father's lead and leave for Dubai. Lulwa graduated and started working as a secretary in Doctor Ali's clinic, but Lulwa was a pride to have as a daughter. She was very respectable, very well-mannered and faithful and even though she was young she was close to God in a special way.

"Mama, I want to wear the *hijab*," she said.

"The Islamic hijab is a good thing but you need to be sure that it's what you want, because changing your mind later on is not an easy thing to do."

"No, Mama, I am sure. I have thought about it for some time now and I am convinced that this is what my heart wants. There is nothing more beautiful, Mama, than obeying God's word, and nothing more honorable than imitating the Prophet's wives and female followers. I want to wear my *hijab* with no regrets whatsoever. I want to win God's love and acceptance of me and this might take me a step closer to Him."

"Go my child. May God bless you in everything you do."

And so she had her hijab on even though some tried to change her mind; peer pressure didn't affect Lulwa in any way. She was ready physically and mentally and I tried to encourage her in any way I could.

Not long after her *hijab* she was proposed to and so married Abdulillah, who was her childhood playmate and who grew to become religious as well. There was a very big wedding, planned by Fatima for Lulwa, but Aisha's mother-in-law, Bibi Gul, passed away only two days before the wedding and they decided to cancel everything out of respect. We had a small henna at our house for the two families and because Abdulillah had just started his career life, my Lulwa was content in sharing his old room with him until God opened the doors of success for my new son-in-law.

Abdulillah was a good man, as I said he was religious, but not to the extent that would make people uncomfortable. He had beauty within him and all those surrounding him saw that beauty in him.

I was happy he married my daughter, I would not have chosen a better man for her.

"*Khala* Khadeeja, I know what Dana did wasn't the right thing but if you really love her than you must forgive her," he said.

"May God have mercy on us."

"*Khala* Khadeeja you are a good woman and you believe in Allah, you have faith. You must understand that this is how God intended it to be."

"I need time."

"Time will only make things worse for both of you. It's also difficult for Dana I am sure of that. She is with a strange man who is now her husband, maybe she is happy but maybe not. Maybe she needs you. She already lost her father; don't let her lose both of you."

I knew that every single word I heard from Abdulillah that day was true. I was angry at my daughter, but she was my daughter at the end of the day. I missed her, her smile, her energy, her humor, everything about her. I missed my baby but I realized a bit too late though for she was already gone. I have lost way too many people in my life and I am not willing to lose more.

*

The years passed by and just as quickly we were planning another wedding for Noor. That was definitely the best thing about having a big family; after every couple of years we planned a wedding.

It was a happy time whenever we planned a wedding. We would all be dancing and singing, the children would enjoy the sweets and the mothers would yell and scream. It was beautiful. There would be happiness again and laugher would fill the air, erasing all marks of sadness. We were one, we were a whole, we completed each other. I was truly proud of my family. I was proud. I was proud that I raised them this way. I was proud that they all shared their joys and tears. I was proud that they all looked after one another; the old cared for the young and the young respected the old. I was proud because whenever I looked at them I saw how much I succeeded in life, after all I have been through. But my Dana was not there and I could not bear it any longer.

"Dear friend, isn't it time to bring Dana back?" whispered Layla's eyes.

She was right, there wouldn't be a better time to see my Dana return and celebrate her sister's wedding.

"But how, how on earth would I ever find her? She is miles away, Layla, miles away, and I am an old woman now. What can I do to bring her back?"

"I am sure you can convince one of your children to go and find her."

Yes, that was a good idea. And the best person for the job was Fatima. Fatima had a strong personality. She always got what she wanted and I was sure after all this time her heart must have softened for her sister. Her husband was a wise man and I knew he would help me convince her that I was right. It wasn't an easy mission but we were able to persuade her in the end. I could even tell from her eyes that she was happy in a way but didn't want to show it. She was never able to hide anything from me, her mother. None of my children could.

*

"Until when am I going to stay like this, dear Lord?" whispered Mohammed during his afternoon prayer.

Since he took that boat to Dubai he was unable to talk about his wife and his children. Even his second wife didn't know much about them. She didn't want to know and tried so hard to make it nothing more than forgotten history.

However, his conscience forced him to relive this history every single day. He was haunted with memories; he was haunted with her love, her smell, her beauty.

He never thought that the day would come where he would be faced with his own son asking about the past, asking about the guilt drawn on his face and his endlessly troubled soul. Why, when his only best friend was the moon and his only love was to the *sujadhh* and *subha*?

At least now he knew that somebody cared, his son cared.

He talked for long hours for he was aching to speak. And his son listened very closely, very carefully. He listened with tears, with pain but with happiness at the same time to know about his big family, a kind and loving one, for he never knew what love was in that house.

It was good to talk, it was good to share a heavy secret, and it was good to know that someone cared.

He watched his son in silence and wished if he could read his mind. He must hate him, he should hate him, but his young weak eyes showed the opposite. A whole night was gone as they spoke, sometimes with words and sometimes in silence.

"What stopped you, Baba, why didn't you go back?"

"I couldn't son, it was too painful."

"But you can't leave them this way, it's not fair."

"You're a good boy, Faisal, there is so much in life you just don't understand."

"But why did you marry Mama?"

"I don't know son, I always thought I knew but I don't."

"Some day you will, someday."

He was hurting for his father, watching him this way. His young heart blamed his mother for he knew she never brought happiness or laughter the way he imagined his step-mother did. She never took care of them or their father and now they were surrounded with nothing but silence, a deadly silence.

"Some day things will be better." he promised his grieving father, "someday the sun will shine again and your heart will rest in peace, Baba."

Mohammed heard his words with stillness. A part of him believed his son and a part of him wanted to run away again and forever.

"I hope so, son, I really do," he heard himself say.

★

Fatima walked down the cold streets of London with her husband, not knowing how to feel. She had been to London so many times but this was different. Her last words to her sister were harsh and now she had to face her all over again; she had to do what seemed at the moment to be impossible and ask for her forgiveness.

Finding Dana wasn't going to be hard, for Dana always wrote to her younger sisters. She took the address from her pocket, looked at it again and then the street sign. Her face was sweating, her heart seemed to run ahead of her, for deep inside she did miss her sister. Her pace was slower and her eyes filled with tears as she saw the small house by the corner. Doctor Ali took her into his arms to calm her but he knew there wasn't much he could do; Fatima had to do it on her own. He knew it was a family thing and he shouldn't interfere. He kissed her on her forehead and walked towards the café at the end of the street, giving her all the time and space she needed.

She walked towards a tree that stood by the house trying to hide herself, stealing peeks from here and there. She could see her sister's shadow moving inside. She saw, and cried trying to think why she ever said such harsh words to her sister. She cried and remembered the first time she walked her to school, the first time she bought her a dress, the first time she read her a story. These were beautiful times, the times they played in their father's lap, the times they sang songs and danced till dawn, the times of happiness and laughter that disappeared from that beautiful house.

She took heavy steps across the garden towards the door, trying to dry her tears and catch her breath. It was before she even realized what was happening Dana was in her arms hugging her, kissing her, and crying. They cried together for a long time, there by the door, in the garden, feeling cold and scared. The past was still there with all its pain but the future was far more promising.

"I waited by this door for so long, wishing one of you would come behind me one day, and just as I was giving up hope you walked in," said Dana in tears.

"I missed you so much, we all did, specially Mama."

"But you all let me go so easily."

"It wasn't easy for us, for any of us. We were all hurting for you but anger was all we felt at the time."

"How is she?"

"She wants you back."

"How could I go back after all that was said to me? Do you know how I felt all this time? Do you know how much I was heartbroken that my own family treated me this way?"

"Dana, it wasn't easy, you know it wasn't, on any of us. But we are family. We have to be together no matter what, we have to stick to each other."

"I wish she had come with you. I wish you'd brought Mama too."

"She is waiting for you."

"I can't leave James."

"Nobody is asking you to leave James, but don't leave Mama either. Too many have done that already; Baba, Nader, Hassan, all of them. She is there waiting for you. Come with me, Dana, only for a few days. I am sure James wouldn't mind."

"What if my brothers won't let me come back?"

"Nobody will stop you, I give you my word. We all have to forget and forgive Dana. We want you to be happy at the end."

They held each other tightly as if in fear of losing each other again and returned to Bahrain together.

"There is nothing like home, nothing at all," whispered Dana, as the plane finally landed in her homeland, in her small island of Bahrain.

*

Dana came home. It was a strange meeting, for even though I was expecting her I wasn't prepared at all; it sure was an emotional reunion.

"Mama," she whispered, "I ached for you, Mama, I missed you so much."

I was speechless yet there was so much I wanted to say, but all I did was cry.

"Don't cry, Mama, I want you to forgive me, I need you to forgive me. I can't live with this guilt inside me, Mama; no matter how much James tried to make me happy I can't get rid of this guilt."

I reached out my shivering hands to her as she ran into my arms and we held and cried for a long time. I could tell everyone was glad. My family was no longer apart, we were all together, the way it should've always been. Two celebrations took place that night, Noor's wedding and Dana's return.

*

It was good to be together again, all of us, but my little family was doomed to scandals. Abdul-Jabbar, who had only been married for three years, was having marital problems. Everyone was suspicious of Fatin's activities but he trusted her blindly, regardless of the problems between them. She would go out late at night and return late, and even though Looloo tried to warn Abdul-Jabbar, he wouldn't believe her, saying it was all crap. I myself tried to warn him about late hanging out with his friends, and therefore paying no attention to what was happening to his life, but he wouldn't listen. Looloo though, known to have the challenging personality, could not sit back and wait like the rest of us.

"I love Abdul-Jabbar too much to watch such a woman take advantage of my brother," she would say angrily.

"Don't interfere with your brother's life, Looloo. He will find out on his own," I tried to calm her.

"No, Mama, I cannot and will not allow her to destroy him. I will find out what this woman is up to and we will put an end to it all."

Fatin's behavior only became weirder, and there was no stopping Looloo, who tried to bring to her brother's attention all the designer clothing and expensive perfumes that he could not afford to buy but were suddenly filling Fatin's closet. I could see his eyes were starting to get skeptical, but his heart was disbelieving it all. He was in a crisis, in a dilemma, but he wouldn't show it.

It was not until a very gloomy day when Abdul-Jabbar received a call from Looloo asking him to call Fatin's brother and meet her in one of the restaurants in a well known street. Abdul-Jabbar rushed to the scene with Mahmoud, Fatin's brother, and Looloo escorted them to a back entrance that led to the apartments on the upper level. Just as they arrived, they found Fatin leaving one of the apartments with a man, a half-naked man, and everything else explained itself.

Fatin never came home after that day. Her things were sent to her along with the divorce papers and I thanked God they had no children between them who would pay the price for such a humiliation.

★

He came home into his empty room and threw himself on the bed. He could hear them whispering outside and buried his face under his pillow for he could take no more. He had had enough and needed peace, only peace.

"How could she do such a thing?" said a voice.

"I knew it would end up this way, I saw it coming, I just did," said another.

"Who does she think she is?"

"Well, she wasn't right for him from the beginning."

Finally there was silence in the house. He was glad they all had left. He hated being the center of attention and he knew that it was going to be the case for a while. He couldn't believe that such a thing had happened to him. His wife, the woman he was with for the past three years, had cheated on him. He wished it had all been a misunderstanding. He wished it was a nightmare but he saw her, with his own eyes. It was real.

"Can I come in now?" In walked the person he wanted most.

She looked tired. Her eyes were red and she looked thin, much thinner than earlier today. She sat next to him watched him breathe heavily and trying to hide his pain.

"You can talk to me you know, I will not judge you. I am your mother."

"What do you want me to say?"

"Tell me you're okay."

"But then I would be lying."

"She wasn't the person for you, you deserve the best."

"Of course, you're my mother, you have to say that."

"No I don't have to say anything."

He looked at her with pain. She looked more hurt than he was. He wanted to comfort her but he needed comfort too. He held her hand and looked at her face with a sad smile.

"I will be alright, Mama, don't worry about me."

"I know you will."

"I loved her."

"I am sure she did too."

"But I don't understand why. I gave her all she ever wanted. I gave her love, passion; I made her live like a queen, I made her dreams come true."

"Some people don't understand these things; they just don't understand how precious they are. You didn't do anything wrong."

"How do you know? What makes you so sure it wasn't my fault?"

"I know you. I know your heart, your kindness. You are one of a kind, you really are."

"How can I face the world?"

"The way I did when your father left. You are not the first or the last who got a divorce. These things happen."

"I still can't believe she did this to me."

"Neither do I, but it happened and you have to face it."

He looked at his mother's face and for the first time felt the pain she went through when his father left her. If she made it alone, in that society, then he was sure to make it too. What was the next step, he didn't know, but he knew something was bound to come up.

Early next morning he walked to the courtroom. He knew he was going to see her for the last time, one more time. What was he to say to her, or should he look away? He was going to divorce her and he wasn't sure if he was able to face all that was happening.

He walked into the tall building and for some reason he felt claustrophobic. She was standing at the end of the corridor with her brother. She was wearing *abaya*, she never wore one before. She hid her eyes with dark glasses. He walked past them into the room where the sheikh was waiting behind his busy desk. The sheikh was a very knowledgeable man. He was known for his wisdom and kindness. This was the same sheikh that had conducted their marriage years ago but now he looked so much older. His white beard came down to his chest and his thick glasses hid the wrinkles around his eyes. His hands were busy shoveling the papers on his desk but his eyes were staring at Abdul-Jabbar.

"Are you sure you want to do this, son?" asked the sheikh.

"It seems like I have no choice, your honor," he answered.

"Now tell me what happened. You know there must be a good reason for me to sign the divorce papers."

He was surprised. He thought that her brother must have said something to the sheikh. He was sure he already knew. It was why he arrived late to the court, he was trying to escape the question, the question of why. He looked around, trying to hold back the tears. He knew he had to say something, he knew he had to say the truth; the truth that would bring humility into his life.

"Adultery," he managed to say.

"You or your wife?" There was more anger in the sheikh's voice.

Your wife. He hated the way it sounded. He wanted to run to a place where no one would know him or ever ask about this wife. A place where no past existed, just a fresh start, and everyone would leave him alone. He looked at the old sheikh and wondered how many men had been in his shoes before? How many men had cheating wives who brought humiliation and pity to their poor husbands? How many divorced their wives for the same reason?

He looked down in sadness and wondered, what did he do wrong? Why hadn't his marriage survived and why did it end this way?

"She cheated, your honor."

"Are you sure she did or you think she did?"

"I saw her, your honor, so did my sister and her brother."

He looked at the sheikh as he called his wife, or ex-wife, and her brother and felt the butterflies in his stomach. His feet were unable to hold him any more and it was about that time when the sheikh asked him to have a seat. He saw her walking in, playing the victim's role, as if he was the one who wronged her. She was crying as she leaned on her brother's shoulder.

"You know your husband is here to divorce you?" asked the sheikh.

She only shook her head in agreement unable to say a word.

"You know the reason?"

"Yes," said her brother on her behalf.

As the sheikh was busy signing the filled forms I looked at the stacks of books in his library trying to avoid looking at her and her brother. It was so funny how it all happened, just yesterday morning they had kissed and hugged, welcoming a new day and whispering love words in each other's ears at breakfast, and the morning after they were broken and hurt signing their divorce papers.

The sheikh was done. He gave an envelope to him and another to her brother. He thanked the sheikh and ran out before anyone could notice his tears. He didn't know where to go or what to do. He wanted to be alone, away from people, away from life, away from reality. There was hate inside him for the first time and for the first time he thought of doing what his father had done before him; go to Dubai.

*

Months passed but my Abdul-Jabbar was never the same again. He was so heartbroken that he couldn't stay in Bahrain any longer. He took the first job offered and flew to Dubai to start a new life there and I couldn't do anything but pray for him.

I didn't even get to enjoy Dana's return seeing another member of my family walk out this way. I knew he needed the distance but it broke my heart. I wondered if he was thinking of seeing his father. I wondered if it was the right time. At least I knew his brother, Faisal, would be with him, my boy would not be alone, but I feared not seeing my son again for that land seems to suck people into not returning, as it did to my Mohammed before.

Chapter Fourteen

"Mama, now that we all met Faisal, and we know where Baba is, we want to go to see him," said Fatima.

"What if he doesn't want to see you?" I asked fearfully.

"We want to take the chance and see for ourselves. Abdurrahman and Mariam are coming as well and we won't take long."

I was too scared that Mohammed might not want to see them. What would happen to them if he rejected them? They had been through enough pain that such a thing might hurt them badly. Who knows what this wife of his had done to him? Who knows how much she changed him. But they were not children any more and I couldn't tell them what to do and what not to do.

I waited for their return impatiently and couldn't wait to hear from them. Surprisingly I still missed Mohammed and still had feelings for him. I knew he didn't deserve anything but he was the first and only man in my life, how could I forget him?

The first thing I noticed was happiness on their faces and I was glad they weren't put down. Abdurrahman looked angry in a way though, but the girls were very emotional.

"Mama, Baba isn't as we expected him to be," Fatima said.

"What do you mean, was he bad to you?"

"No, not at all, but he wasn't in a good condition. They live in a small apartment in a very poor area and he was sick. He couldn't move much and everything had to be done for him," said Mariam.

I was surprised myself, a small apartment in a poor area? Whatever happened to that lady's money which he married her for? And why was he sick? He was still considered young to be in a condition where everything had to be done for him.

"What about his wife?"

"Her name is Amina; she was both nice and evil. But we have two beautiful sisters, more beautiful than Faisal had described," said Fatima.

"Baba is paying for what he did to us," said Abdurrahman, "maybe it's time we forgave him."

I saw guilt in Abdurrahman's eyes. He has been so angry at his father all these years and watching him in a poor condition made him feel blameworthy. He told me once that if they had found him earlier he wouldn't be so sick by now and even though I tried to explain things for him he couldn't rest his aching heart.

"How is Abdul-Jabbar? Did he see his father?"

"He is good, still angry and hurt but he will be fine. Not yet; he just wasn't ready, it's all a matter of time," said Fatima.

"How is Faisal?" I asked, concerned.

"He is pretty much the same," said Abdurrahman.

"This man has so much faith inside him, although he knows he's dying he is content. His smile is always on his face and his laughter made our trip a memorable one," said Mariam.

Fatima and doctor Ali decided to take Mohammed to Mecca and left right away after Doctor Ali took all the medical equipment needed for Mohammed's travel. Sheikh Abdurrahman, Doctor Ali's father, decided to join in as well, and Fatima was sure that it would please her father too. I wished I could go with them; I wanted to see Mohammed, but I couldn't ask and they didn't offer. And I kept on wondering, now that they know where their father is would I ever get to see him again? Would he come back? Has the time finally come?

*

He could not believe it. A handsome young man, two beautiful young ladies sitting in front of him, filled with love, with passion. They were nicely dressed; more than nicely dressed, they were in a good state as if the world had spread them with all its riches.

"Abdurrahman, Fatima and Mariam," they introduced themselves.

He wanted to cry but couldn't. He wanted to run to hold them, but couldn't. He wanted to scream out words of joy, ask about the love of his life, beg them to take him back but he couldn't. For the first time in his life Mohammed was ashamed, embarrassed and he let his head down and gave a sad laugh.

Fatima couldn't hold herself. She walked towards him in both fear and happiness. She lifted his face, kissed his forehead and held his hand tight. When she saw the first tears in her father's eyes she hugged him and cried. He cried. Abdurrahman cried. Mariam cried. They each took turns in hugging their father and they talked. They talked about the past, about the future. Mohammed saw them sitting by him and he ached for their mother. He wanted to ask but was afraid. He knew it was too late.

He remembered them so well, when they were children. He remembered their naughtiness, their humor, beautiful things they took from their mother. He remembered them running into his arms as he walked in the door, as they did now, and he remembered the goodbye kiss the day he left. How much they had grown up, how amazing they turned out to be. He wondered now even more, more than he ever wondered, how did she do it? How did she survive all alone to raise such wonderful children? Did she marry another? Could she forget all about him and marry another for his money, as he did?

He was dirty. He was forgotten in his old chair, unable to move, unable to help himself, and his three children could not leave their father like that. Mariam and Fatima bathed him while Abdurrahman went to buy him some new clothes. The stepsisters were welcoming. They were shy, even embarrassed, but were not allowed to stay in the room for a long time. Amina was envious. She was trying to be nice, and Mohammed saw how fake her expressions were. If one of her daughters started a conversation with Mariam or Fatima she would make up an excuse and call them out of the room. She had for so long imagined Khadeeja and her daughters as beggars after Mohammed left them and seeing them in their best was shocking, more than shocking. She was even more angry at Mohammed now, even accused him of sending them her money.

He didn't want them to leave, or maybe he wanted to leave with them. He watched them walk out the door and he cried. He wanted to call them but his voice was nowhere to be found. Were they ever coming back? He didn't know. Yes, he was being selfish. Though he had left them behind for many years he didn't want them to leave him now. Yes, he shouldn't have left in the first place.

★

"Mama, can I stay with you for some time? Only until I decide what I want to do?" Noor shocked me one fine day.

"What is that supposed to mean?"

"Nothing really, please don't worry, I am just confused and I don't know what to do."

"Noor, is there something you want to tell me, dear? Is there something you are hiding? You know I don't want to interfere with your life but if you need to talk, please, I am here."

"He has changed, Mama, everything about him has changed. Life with him seems impossible all of a sudden."

"You had a fight?"

"It's not the first time. It's stupid. He doesn't like anything I do, he objects to everything I say. Sometimes I think I made a mistake, a big one, the day I married him."

"Now come here dear, you are angry now; it's no time to talk. You are probably saying things you don't really mean. Let's call it a night, shall we? We can talk more tomorrow when you are calm."

I went into my bedroom concerned. This wasn't the first time they had had a fight and I was sure it wasn't going to be the last either. Could something really be wrong with their relationship?

"Can I sleep here?" I heard her say.

"Of course, come here next to me."

She slept like a child. As I looked at her confused little face I realized how quickly the time passed. I remembered when she broke her leg, how the children were around her, how they sang to her, read to her, fed her and did all they could to make her feel comfortable. And now she was here on my bed, hurt all over again, but this time with a broken heart. Would her brothers and sisters comfort her now the way they did before? Would we even be able to comfort her in the first place? I remembered the day I walked her to school for the first time. I remembered the day she ran into the house announcing her graduation. I remembered how nervous she was the first day of college. She always did what she believed was the right thing, even if we tried to convince her otherwise. When she was proposed to by her husband, I tried to explain to her that he might not be the best choice. They were both very young and they were both at the same age. Times have changed. They were both immature. It was also a fact that women matured before men. It would be a difficult relationship if the wife was more mature than the husband. It was also another fact that women aged faster than men. But she wouldn't listen. She decided that he was the man for her. It was a fairy tale, every little girl's fairy tale. Her prince would come to rescue her, to make all her dreams come true, to make her his princess. He was what every girl wanted. To her he was muscular, he was handsome, he was a man, but to me he was nothing but a child. Yet this child came from a kind family and they loved her so much. I tried to make her see, but the idea of marrying this man was so beautiful to her that everything else didn't matter. So they got married and like every fairy tale they were supposed to live happily ever after, but that didn't happen. As soon as they came back from the honeymoon the problems started and somehow they never stopped. This was the new generation. They never listen to the older generation. They considered all our advice, all our thoughts and beliefs to be old fashioned. And when things go wrong they run back into our arms for protection. What am I going to do with her, what would I say to make her feel better? I decided to leave it to her. She had to learn to take care of herself and decide her own fate. She had to learn to become independent for I would not always be around to protect her. I was sure she would make the right decision no matter what it would be.

Three days passed. She didn't call him and he didn't call her. I watched her jump every time the phone rang. I watched her cry. I watched her taking off her wedding band and then wearing it again. I watched her pray. I had to do something.

"Hello, Lulwa, I need to speak to you. It's very urgent but it has to be somewhere else other than the house."

"Is everything okay?"

"You will understand when I see you."

"I will send the driver in an hour. Come to my house, I am alone today."

Lulwa was waiting by the door. She has always been the mature one, the one I trusted the most. She was wise, intelligent and sensible, and I knew she was the right person to tell. I knew she wouldn't tell a living soul.

"Mama, what happened?"

"Nothing, just the usual. Your sister, Noor, and her husband had another fight."

"And?"

"This time she took her things and came home."

"Oh my God, they haven't even finished a year together."

"I told you they were both young and immature."

"Who knows about it?"

"No one but you, and you should keep it a secret."

"You have something in mind?"

"Yes. I think you should speak to this child and see what his problem is. Our girl is not a toy; he either straightens up and behaves, or leaves her. She has her family to take care of her. It's been three days and he hasn't even called. She is going crazy and I have to do something. I will not allow anyone do this to my little girl. I will not allow him to disrespect her or treat her like she is nothing."

"Calm down, Mama. I don't think it's to that extent. As you said before, they are children."

"Will you do it?"

"If you think it's the only way, yes I will, but I will not threaten him or ask him to leave her. I will only try to understand what the problem really is."

Lulwa called and I was trying to overhear the conversation but at this age I hardly heard a thing. They talked for almost an hour until she finally walked towards me, laughing.

"You were right, they were children, Mama."

"What happened?"

"Did Noor tell you what started their fight?"

"No, I didn't ask her."

"He wanted pizza and she wanted sandwiches so they disagreed and she left the house."

"Over pizza and sandwiches?"

"Imagine that!"

We laughed so hard and I rushed home, for I felt like slapping Noor. Lulwa came with me and we found her as I had left her; in front of the television with the phone right next to her.

"Crazy little girl, get up at once and pack your stuff. You left your husband over pizza and sandwiches?"

"You spoke to him? What did he say?"

"He is coming tonight to pick you up, and you better have pizza ready for him," said Lulwa, as we burst into laughter all over again.

"Oh, so it's funny to you, huh?" as she started laughing too.

Noor went back to her house the fourth night and promised me to think before acting. Lulwa and I laughed every time we remembered the incident and I was glad it had all ended up this way. To be honest I was afraid things like that would still come up between the two and they would act in foolish matter, but I was also certain that their love would save them at the end of the day.

Chapter Fifteen

When Doctor Ali and Fatima returned from Mecca, Looloo gave a proposal announcement, and even though we were all happy at first, the surprise came a day later that made some of us pretty sad and others angry. It turned out to be that even though Essa, Looloo's man, wanted her so much and was ready to do anything for her, his mother did not want such a marriage to take place and would do anything to stop it. This was going to be another marriage catastrophe.

"You will not marry this man; if they don't want us we don't want them," screamed Abdurrahman.

"What is our fault? Why should we pay the price because the families don't get along?" cried Looloo.

"You mean to tell me that you will marry him even though his mother promised to ruin such a marriage?" asked Fatima.

"Essa promised me that he will not allow it; she will learn to accept me," said Looloo.

"But how? Don't you have any pride? Besides, what will people say?" said Mariam.

"Leave her now," I demanded, "let me speak to her privately, go to your houses; I will be the person to make the decision. I have had enough already and I lost Dana once, I am not going to lose another now."

I was so angry that they all left with no word said. I was finally alone with Looloo to hear the whole story.

"I met him at work, Mama. It's funny, a long story that somehow turned to a fairy tale," she said.

"I am all ears, I want to hear everything. The decision is yours to make but I won't give you my blessing unless I am convinced."

"I had always heard about him when I was in college. He was known to be the grouchy man, very dignified, very arrogant. I never saw him though, but fate brought us to the same place after graduation and we have been working together for four years now. At first, I hated him, not that he was a bad person, but because I had that picture about him from college in my head."

"And how did he prove you wrong?"

"Working with him made me see a side many never saw. He was a good hearted man, very honorable, very trustworthy. I soon learned that people looked at his shy unique personality as weird but it is very beautiful once you get to know it. I enjoyed working with him; he was helpful and kind and our relationship grew from friendship to love."

"And how do you know he is serious? How do you know it is true love?"

"Mama, he has been out of Bahrain for a whole year now. He was sent to the States for a course but he couldn't stay any longer. We need each other, Mama, you don't understand how much we are already attached."

"What about his mother? What is her problem?"

"His mother is not a Bahraini. She is from Dubai and was hoping that Essa would be marrying her niece. Somehow she doesn't like the Bahraini girls, or maybe just preferred her own nationality, but this is the only reason she rejected me."

"But she has promised to ruin this marriage no matter what?"

"Yes, but Essa isn't a child and he won't listen to her."

"Baby, there is something you need to understand. All men, regardless of what they say or promise, side up with their mothers more than their wives. The mother always finds a way to convince her son and interfere directly or indirectly. After all, she's been around him longer and knows exactly how to get to him. Besides, Looloo, you don't want to come between a mother and her son, you don't want to cause problems or be the reason for a family break up or feud."

"But Essa knows his mother more than any of us and he assures me that she will give up and learn to love me."

"You deserve more, Looloo, you know that."

"I want him, Mama. I am not a child any more, I am twenty-six. My sisters got married much younger and I am ready for a family. I am sure of this man and I want him more than anything. If he is ready to fight for me than I am ready to fight for him."

"I will give you my blessing, Looloo, but I am not happy. I am not comfortable with his mother and I don't want to see you heartbroken. I did my part and I warned you. The rest is in your hands, do as you wish."

And so the wedding took place only a week after. We didn't even have enough time to prepare for anything. Looloo took care of it all, the catering, the music, the invitations. She did not want anyone to do anything but attend, and for the first time we had a mixed wedding, men and women all together; she was stubborn and wanted it that way no matter what we told her. She had brought a big tent that used the rest of Fatima's land and hired some company to decorate it with lights and all that stuff. I wasn't sure if I was happy or angry or sad so I decided to go with the flow and prayed for patience. I was an old woman, I couldn't take any more worries in my life.

The wedding was a disaster for many reasons. Let's see; first of all there was a partition between the band and the guests that fell directly on the band and broke one of their instruments. You could imagine how angry they were and how badly they sang after that. Then the food didn't show up, and as Dana and Lulwa looked for the caterers all over Bahrain they finally arrived with only half the order, so some people didn't get to have their dinner after all. Just as it was time to cut the cake, Essa's mother made an entrance and ordered a table covered from all sides so that she wouldn't be sitting with the men. She was objecting to everything and her hurtful comments were pretty loud. Everyone started to leave early and Essa took Layla and went to a hotel where they would be staying for their first couple of nights.

"Mama, we are going to the States, to Chicago." Looloo surprised me early next morning.

"Chicceego? Where is that? And why?"

"Chicago, Mama, Chicago. Essa wants to finish his course and I want to go with him."

"But Looloo, what about your work? My God, you keep on surprising me with new things every day."

"It's life, Mama, you never know what to expect."

I knew I couldn't stop her, she was married now, even though my heart didn't want her to leave. She was my little baby, the youngest in the house. What would I do without her? It was only then when it occurred to me how time went by so quickly and I was too busy to even notice it. When did they all grow up to be men and women? Mothers and fathers? How did I survive life when it was so mean to me and so unfair? Where have I reached and what am I going to do now? I was never so alone as after Layla's marriage. I missed the full house and my busy life trying to make a living for all of them. All I could do now was thank the Lord for all that he had rewarded me, and wait for what was yet to come.

★

"Faisal is dead," shouted Fatima, after receiving a phone call one day as we were all sitting in the garden.

He died only a month after they had visited, leaving behind a beautiful fiancée, a mother, two sisters, and a sick father, who all depended on him. Upon the news Aisha, Fatima, Mariam, and Abdurrahman all left for Dubai to attend the funeral, and even though I wanted to go so badly I knew it wasn't the right time to show up. I was grieving for him. I grieved for my husband's son from his second wife, the one I despised for ruining my life, not knowing if she was at fault or Mohammed. But the children were not to blame for anything. I loved them with all my heart. My children were happy they had two sisters and a brother and I accepted them as members of my own family. They did have Mohammed's blood running through their veins. Today a son died, my son died, and I had every right to grieve for him. May Allah rest his soul.

"Mama, would you like to see Baba?" Abdurrahman asked me the day he returned from Dubai.

"I don't know, son, I don't know."

"Well, he is here he is in Bahrain and is staying in my house for a while."

That was shocking news. Mohammed, my Mohammed, the one I have been waiting for nearly thirty years now finally came back. But how was I going to see him? How was he going to meet me? Had he forgotten me and all that was between us? Did he still love me as I loved him? The news made me go all the way back to the night of my wedding. I relived the same feeling, the feeling of fear, excitement, and curiosity.

"Take care of yourself. Don't be afraid. I know for sure that you will be happy baby. Be good to your husband, obey him. Do all that pleases him and so he'll do the same. Remember, Khadeeja, all that I taught you and I will always be here for you," Mama told me that night and I wondered if she was still alive what would she have said?

"I want you to see him, come with me please, I am sure he will be happy to see you and I know you never stopped waiting for him," continued Abdurrahman.

And so I did. I walked to my room as if it was my wedding night but instead of Mama I heard Abdurrahman's call from behind the door while I put on my *abaya* at a snail's pace. Though he was my husband, he was my Mohammed, I insisted on wearing the *abaya*. I insisted on meeting him formally; besides I was also very shy. Layla was in my hands, reliving the past all over again with me. With me as she has always been.

I was scared, didn't know what to expect in there. I walked very slowly towards the living room until Abdurrahman ran out of patience and pulled me in with him.

I closed my eyes and there I was again, behind the wooden doors on my wedding night. I could still hear the women's slippers as they walked away and I could feel him there.

And then came the first touch. He left his hand resting on mine as he led me to the room. I didn't know what to feel, I was scared, I was shy, but mostly I was curious. I wanted to know who was the man holding my hand, what did he look like and what would my life with him be. His touch was warm, his voice was sweet, and I could already feel his good vibe.

But this time it was different. There was no good vibe, there was anger, there was sadness.

There he was but I could only watch through the corner of my eyes. I was too shy to lift my head up, even though I tried to look as confident and dignified as possible. I felt angry when I first set my foot in the room and was filled with regret for listening to Abdurrahman. The pain this man caused me seemed to come back at that instant and I wanted to walk out. He should come to me, why should I go to him? He was the one who walked out on me and so he should earn my forgiveness. That is, if he wanted it anyway.

"Mama, this is Baba," said Abdurrahman, and he left the room, closed the door behind him, and I was alone with Mohammed all over again. Something I definitely didn't see coming though I felt it and prayed for it.

"Khadeeja?" I heard him say heavily. His voice was as sweet and as gentle as it had always been and as I heard it again after thirty years I realized I had missed him more than I thought I did.

"Would you come sit next to me?" he asked.

I didn't move. I stood where I was, staring at the floor with so much running through my head.

"Would you at least let me look at you?" he begged.

It was as if I was waiting for the right moment to look at him, see him with my two eyes to believe that it was really him after all. I lifted my head slowly and with tearful eyes managed to see what was remaining of my Mohammed. My God, what happened to him? Where did his handsome face and muscular body go? He was worse than the kids described. Sickness was all over his face and it just wasn't my Mohammed any more.

"You are so beautiful, more beautiful than when I left you. How stupid was I, Khadeeja, how stupid was I to leave an angel?"

"You caused me so much pain," I said, without even thinking of what to say.

"Forgive me, Khadeeja, please forgive me."

"You caused me so much pain." And I cried. I cried so much that I did not even notice the kids walk in and try to comfort me. I cried so much I didn't not notice that Mohammed was crying even more.

"Hello, Khadeeja," I heard a strange voice say.

I raised my head towards the voice and it was her, his second wife, Amina. What was she doing here? I didn't know, and she had the guts to even walk in and talk to me!

"Hello," I said in a rather unwelcoming tone.

"May I speak to you privately please?"

I stood up and left the room as she walked behind me and went to the guest room to listen to what she had to say, just out of curiosity. I wanted more time with Mohammed but I knew she couldn't bear the thought of me sitting alone with her husband.

I looked at her for the very first time. She was tall and thin, bony in a way. She had no beauty; she wasn't ugly but not beautiful in any way. Her hair was curly and short and her eyes had no passion in them. She was a tough woman, an angry woman who now felt defeated. I felt nothing towards her, not even hatred, for now I had it all. After all this time I had it all over again.

"Khadeeja, I know this is weird, I know neither of us is comfortable, but there are other things that are important and we should take into account."

"Such as?"

"Mohammed has a heart problem that only got worst with Faisal's death. His legs are already paralyzed and the doctors believe he needs all the help he can get emotionally to overcome the shock of his son's death and the effects it had on his health."

"Why are you telling me this?"

"We have one thing in common and that is the wellbeing of Mohammed. And with both of us here we have to at least try to get along to make sure that we don't cause more emotional problems."

"Look, Amina, I have nothing against you. Mohammed left many years ago and I nearly forgot him. To me he is nothing but the father of my children and it ends there. And if I do something to help Mohammed emotionally then I will do it for only one reason and that is for my children. They have been wanting him in their lives for so long, and now that he is finally here they deserve to have some good memories with him."

"Then we have an understanding."

I knew she didn't care about Mohammed. I knew she wanted me to stay away but I also knew that I owned his heart from day one and always have since then. I knew no matter how hard she tried she would never succeed, and I needed to be with Mohammed. It was my right to know why he left.

I left the room to be welcomed by another young lady whom I guessed to be either Badriya or Latifa.

"*Khala* Khadeeja, I am so happy to finally meet you. I have heard so much from my sisters about you."

"And I have heard so much about you too, but which one are you?"

"I am Latifa the youngest."

"The naughtiest, as I heard."

She let out a cute laugh that made me notice how much she looked like Lulwa. Yes, she was their sister and my daughter in a way, for we managed to become really good friends in no time.

As the days passed I saw Mohammed's love blooming again. His eyes would shine when I walked in and his smile wouldn't leave his face. But we could never be alone; there was always Amina there and I knew she made him feel uncomfortable in a way. It was already time for Latifa's school to restart and so they had to leave as we all thought, but Mohammed and Abdurrahman had another plan.

"My father is not going anywhere. My father is staying here in his home, in his house," said Abdurrahman.

"Yes, he is right, I don't want to go back there. I am finally where I always wanted to be," he said as he looked at me straight in the eye.

"But Mohammed, you leave us there who will take care of us?" cried Amina.

"*Khala* Amina, don't forget the condition I found Baba in and don't tell me that you were depending on him, or that his existence even matters to you," said Abdurrahman.

She had nothing to say after that comment and I learned later on how Mohammed was left in a very poor condition after Faisal's death. Faisal was his only caretaker. Nobody would change him, bathe him, or even feed him. He was like a statue left in a corner and forgotten about, but that wasn't going to be the case any more. Mohammed made the decision and he wanted to stay even though Amina tried so hard to change his mind. She only ended up leaving alone with Latifa, who was convinced that her father was better off in Bahrain.

"If I was older and stronger I would have taken care of Baba, but I am only a little girl, completely under Mama's control," said

Latifa sadly. "I wish I had a mother like you. Baba really didn't know your worth when he left you."

★

He saw her, the love of his life, the only love. Yes she was old but so beautiful, more than he had remembered. He had imagined her growing old for so many years but not this way, not so lovely. Her eyes still had that naughty twinkle, her hair was still long, it's black and silver silk threads fell softly on her shoulder and he longed to touch it again. She still had her shy smile, her skin was that of a child yet the years had left some wrinkles which only added to her beauty. Her walk was still graceful, her voice was still attractive. The years had given her so much confidence, so much did she go through, so much did she learn.

Now he loved her even more, he felt even more guilty. She had it all. Everything they dreamed of together.

How did they all welcome him like that, with open arms, no bad feelings, no blaming or accusing, nothing? He wished someone would scream at him, asking him about the past, asking him to leave, but all this love was impossible.

He cried. It was all he could do. He had left with all his strength and they took him back with all his weakness. What a world, what a world.

★

Keeping Mohammed in Abdurrahman's house was becoming too difficult for Abdurrahman's wife who had to entertain a full house every day, especially while taking care of her young children, so I offered that Mohammed come to stay with me, for the house was big and I was all alone. I also needed to be with Mohammed on my own. I wanted to see what it would feel like, what would happen. I was like a child seeking an adventure, and God knows how much I needed it. I could see how delightful the news was to him and I couldn't hide my happiness either. The day I longed for had finally arrived. Mohammed was back after all these years and I welcomed him with an open heart and a forgiving soul.

With Mohammed's arrival at my house I received another news. Looloo came back from Cheecagi or where ever she was, with a big stomach ahead of her. She was six months' pregnant and came directly from the airport to see me.

"Mama, I missed you so much! You can't believe the times I cried on Essa's shoulders, wanting to return just to see you," she cried as she hugged me.

"Oh, my baby, you look wonderful! Tell me, Looloo, are you happy?"

"Oh, Mama, more than I ever expected."

"Good, then, Looloo, would you sit down, there are some new things going on here, new changes."

"What happened, is everything alright?"

"Oh yes, it is. Your father is here. He is inside in the bedroom. He lives here now and, well, don't you want to meet him? I know it's difficult after all this time, but you never saw your father. Isn't it time you met him?"

I could see how surprised she was but she was not happy. She was shocked and hurt and her face turned red with emotion.

"No!" she said angrily. "He didn't care that you were pregnant with me, he just left. I didn't matter to him, why should he matter to me now?"

"Looloo, your father is sick and he regrets the past," I said shocked, expecting my daughter to be excited by finally meeting her father for the first time and after all these years of wondering about him.

"I can't forget nor forgive. Sorry, Mama, but Essa is waiting for me." she ran out the door and I didn't know what to tell Mohammed.

I understood why Looloo was angry, I know she felt unwanted by her father. I didn't know how to make her meet him, for I was sure that he would change her mind and start forming a relationship, one that was never there before. Even though Mohammed was disappointed at Looloo's refusal of him he didn't give up. It was a sunny day and Mohammed had asked for a wheelchair to help him move around the house easily. Looloo stopped by to say hello, knowing that her father was always in the bedroom, but Mohammed surprised her as he managed to sit on the wheelchair with Fatima and Mariam's help. He asked to be alone with Looloo and they sat in the living room for a very long time, but whatever he told her that day it worked. Looloo was the most attached to her father and his favorite too.

It was a full house every day. All who knew Mohammed came to see him and he was surrounded with his children, grandchildren, and even great-grandchildren. He was surrounded with so much love, passion, and respect that it only added to his guilt even though it made him happy.

The best times was at night when the house would be empty again and Mohammed and I would sit back and talk about all the years that passed.

"I bet you are wondering why I left you, Khadeeja," he told her one night.

"I heard many stories but couldn't get myself to believe them."

"I never thought you would be so loyal to me all these years though I never even wrote to you. I was expecting your brothers to write to me asking for divorce papers even though I prayed no such thing would happen. I left you but somehow couldn't divorce you."

"But why, Mohammed, what did I do wrong?"

"That was the whole problem. You didn't do anything wrong. You were a beautiful angel and still are. I was the one to blame. I wasn't good enough for you and I was surrounded with really bad people who encouraged me to go behind money and forget my values."

"I wish you had said something before you left."

"I wish I had never left."

I looked into his eyes and saw years and years of regret. I saw pain, I saw sadness and I thought to myself, he paid the price. There was no need to blame him any more, he went through enough.

"Tell me, Khadeeja, how did you survive?"

"I went through a lot, Mohammed. Nothing was easy. Life was difficult and we were always on the edge. We were poor but filled with pride and built ourselves from nothing. At first I had to write to Hassan, who left all his life behind to come help me raise my big family, and he stayed with us till he died a few years later.

After that Fatima sacrificed her own education to work and keep her sisters and brothers in school, and soon after the others graduated and we had more income. God kept rewarding me and gave me good sons-in-law. Doctor Ali gave me a land and helped Dana, Abdurrahman, and Abdul-Jabbar build this house you see today. It was a difficult life but I am happy now, I am comfortable and content watching my grandchildren growing in my arms."

Mohammed cried. Never have I seen a tortured soul and even though I tried to calm him down, his repentance was taking over what remained of him. His sickness was getting worse and I prayed for his wellbeing. I wasn't ready to let go of him. I wasn't at all.

"She was not good to me, Amina. Or maybe I wasn't good to her. I don't know. All I knew was that my body was in Dubai and my heart was with you. You were all I could think of but I couldn't get myself to return. I thought you would throw me out, I got myself to believe that you hated me that you didn't even want to look at my face and so I stayed in hell and never got to taste happiness or love again."

"Didn't you have any faith in my love for you?"

"Oh Khadeeja, I have hurt you so badly. I didn't know if the love I saw from you would ever be the same."

"But you have good children, amazing characters who took all that was kind from you."

"Yes, they were good, I couldn't be a good father to them though. I was always running away from Amina and so ended up spending few hours at home, until I got sick and was forced to retire. Even then I sunk into a neverending silence that killed me even more."

"You are home now and that is what counts."

"Yes I am, and it sure feels good."

Chapter Sixteen

"Wake up, wake up," cried Lulwa softly as she tried to wake me up.

"What time is it?" I asked.

"Mama, it's around 4 a.m. Don't be frightened, but we are all here in the house."

"What's going on? What happened?"

"Kuwait has been invaded, Mama. Don't be frightened but all neighboring countries are threatened and are on alert."

"What do you mean, invaded?"

"Iraq took over the country. We are here now, I just thought of telling you."

I forced myself out of bed and there they were, watching the news at 4 a.m. It was August 1990; the Iraqi troops entered Kuwait by surprise and threatened any country who tried to help the Kuwaitis. We watched the invasion on TV and it was sad. The Kuwaitis fled their own country; they left their own homes, their properties and ran for their lives. Those caught by the invaders were tortured and abused. The women were raped and the children lost their innocence. We watched it everyday on TV like a soap opera and we prayed for them.

The world wasn't allowing me to rejoice my husband's return. War. In our lands, the Arabian lands, between the Muslims. What was going to happen next? Instead of delight and excitement for Mohammed's return, the house was filled with anxiety. We would hum a prayer or cry in silence as we watched how brutal things were on TV.

There wasn't much we could do to help them, the Kuwaitis I mean. The government tried to supply those who arrived with housing, schools, food, and emotional support. The buildings, cars, and walls were covered with flags and maps of Kuwait but things only worsened.

As the whole world interfered we all waited with horror for the war, the Gulf War. The United States of America and its allies had been threatening Iraq to withdraw its troops or face a military attack but the threatening left no results. It was bound to happen and we were waiting for it.

"Mama, here, keep these, we need to stack them in a safe place," cried Fatima, as she brought in boxes and boxes of canned food.

"What is all this, child? Are we throwing a party? Can't you see what's going on in the world?"

"Oh, Mama, we have to be prepared. What do you think we'll eat when the war starts and we have to lock ourselves up in the house? You should see the supermarkets, people are buying anything they can put their hands on."

She was right. People were freaking out. They bought anything and everything. There was a shortage of food and supplies already and prices were on the rise. My house alone turned, to a supermarket. They all did their share of buying and I did mine by storing them safely. There was all you could think of; batteries, bottled water, all kinds of canned foods, biscuits, tissue, scotch tapes, ropes, gas masks, a small cooker, soap, first aid kit and much more.

"We have to cover the windows," said Abdurrahman.

"Yeah, all of them, including the bathroom windows," said Looloo.

"What now?" I asked.

"Well!" they looked at each other, "it's nothing to worry about it's just precautions," said Abdurrahman.

"Why do you want to cover the windows?" I insisted.

"Iraq has chemical weapons and now it's threatening to use them if America attacks," explained Looloo.

"And what are these chemical weapons?"

"They are like bombs that spread this deathly gas and it stays in the air, polluting it for a while."

Imagining what such a weapon could do to us brought a shiver to my body and I rushed into the storage area to bring the Scotch tape and ropes. The children covered all the windows with heavy-duty nylon and stacked more to cover the doors in case we faced such an attack. All my children came to stay with me, including their own little families. Though the house wasn't big enough for all of us, we all loved it and Mohammed was the happiest father all over again.

It was January 1991 when the news spread like fire, the United States of America attacked Iraq. We woke up to a loud siren that spread all over Bahrain to warn people for no one knew what was going to happen next. Everyone woke up and ran to the TV and there it was the start of the Gulf War.

"I feel bad for them," said Lulwa, sadly.

"Yeah, I know. The Iraqi people shouldn't be punished for what the government was doing," said one of Fatima's daughters.

"What will happen to them?" Mariam's daughter asked her.

It was all on TV, the whole thing. We could see the bombs as they came down on Iraq and we could see the frightened city of Baghdad burning. We silently grieved for the people. We grieved for Islam. And we grieved for the unity of the Arabs that will never return to our region.

The sirens continued for weeks and the air strikes were nonstop. The prayers echoed from mosques for both the Kuwaiti and Iraqi people. Organizations collected money, food, medicine and clothes. Schools and universities stopped and the offices, buildings, and hospitals had to build their own chemical-proof rooms, enough for their occupants. We lived in an emergency state and though it was frightening, it woke people up from their materialistic dreams to face reality and the harsh world they lived in.

Sometimes we even laughed at the condition we were living in. We would all be enjoying our tea when all of a sudden we would hear the sirens and everybody would run in confusion. The women ran for their children, the men covered the doors and I would open the tap to fill the tub with water before any chemical could force us to stop using tap water.

Through all that we went through at that time I could not help think how God wanted Mohammed to be with us in such a time. God wanted him to feel all his children surrounding him, to spend quality time with them, to make it up in a way. Though he was sick he would force himself to stay up, only to cherish the moments and relive his past, before he took that boat. It was a gift from God and he knew he didn't deserve it but God was the most merciful, most gracious.

A few weeks later Iraq retreated and the war came to an end. We were able to remove the nylon again but the air around us was so polluted that we decided to leave them on. There was no chemical attack but the burning wells of Kuwaiti oil were affecting us too. The rain would leave black spots everywhere, animals and plants died, and the children were continuously sick.

The American army, who came in thousands to Bahrain during the war, were still around. It reminded me of the British rule period, but this time it seemed like an indirect colonization. But people were happy the war was over, they wanted a moment of peace; they were too desperate for peace to realize the new colonization.

*

I was worried about Mohammed. He was giving up on life I could see it in his eyes. His sickness only worsened in the following few months. He lost use of his body from the chest all the way down and only some of us could understand what he was saying. Abdul-Jabbar quit his job and returned home to stay with his father now that it was more difficult for me to take care of him alone, and Looloo was in charge of his food and medication. Even though he slept for long hours during the day he still wanted me next to him the whole time. He loved watching me hold his hand even though he wouldn't feel anything, but it seemed like his heart felt every move. He was like a small child all over again. He longed for love and security. He longed for being wanted and always surrounded with his children and grandchildren like the good old days. He wanted to forget his past and hoped for a peaceful death. His eyes were an open book, a book that he could never hide from me.

*

He was dying. He knew he was dying. But he was happy. It had been a long time since he felt that way. There were even times when he forgot the past, forgot that he ever left. They were always with him now, laughing, singing, recalling the past.

He was with Khadeeja again. It was all that mattered. She had welcomed him back he was in her house, their house all over again. He was clean, in a clean place. He would watch her decorate the room with fresh flowers every day to welcome the many guests, she would sing, she would tease, and he would love. He was ready to go. He knew he was forgiven and he was ready to leave again but this time a good leave, not running away, not hiding from the truth, this time he would go to his resting place where guilt, pain, humiliation, and injustice did not exist.

Peace. He had waited his whole life for peace. He was old, he was sick; he was content and ready to die.

They all grew up to be wonderful men and women, he was proud. He was proud of his loyal wife. He was proud of her strength, her faith, her heart.

He was longing for Nader and Faisal for he knew they were somewhere waiting for him, calling him. He searched the room for the angel of death. He knew he would be able to see him when the time came. He felt him there already, just waiting for the ticking time to stop. He felt the coldness of the grave and the warmth of Allah's forgiveness. He wondered if they would miss him, if they would cry, if she would cry.

"Yes, she will," he told himself, "my love will cry for me."

Chapter Seventeen

It was November 8, 1992. I woke up for *fajr* prayer. It was still dark outside. I heard a weird mumbling so I walked towards the windows to make sure they were closed properly when I realized that the mumbling was coming from Mohammed. I turned on the lights and there he was, pale and cold.

"Mohammed, are you feeling alright? Are you cold?" It was even harder for me to understand a word from him this time. "Let me go call Abdul-Jabbar and I will be right back."

His eyes were filled with tears and his voice was all cracked up as he tried to say something.

"No, Khadeeja, stay, I want to talk to you."

"You are tired. We can talk later, let Abdul-Jabbar get a doctor."

"No, there is no time left, I am dying and I want to die, let me go in peace."

"You have so much ahead of you, you are not dying tonight." I struggled to keep myself from crying as I prayed for God's help and mercy.

"Forgive me."

"Mohammed what are you saying? We already talked about the past and threw everything behind our back."

"Forgive me. Say it. I want to hear it from you. I want you to say it," he begged.

"I forgive you; you know that I forgive you."

"You have been such a good wife, so loyal, so pure. You have always been the love of my life; no matter what people said you were always the person I loved and it will be that way. But tell me, Khadeeja, do you love me?"

"Do I love you? Why do you think I waited all these years when every thing around me convinced me that you were never coming back? Why do you think I had my heart and my home wide open, welcoming you back? You are my husband, the father of my children, how can I not love you?"

"Even after all that I did to you?"
"Even after all that you did to me."
"I am ready to leave now. I am ready to bid you all farewell."

He spoke slower and heavier but looked more serene than ever. I wanted to go call someone but I sat there staring at him and felt my heart tearing into two. The most difficult thing was watching him die; I had to see him leave me all over again as we both hummed a silent prayer.

"Let me die in your arms," he said.

I struggled to lift his head up and managed to rest him on my chest, holding him close to me, feeling him take his last breaths.

"You are more beautiful than I had ever imagined," he said, and closed his eyes forever.

Mohammed died in my arms and I couldn't let go. I rocked him and cried until Abdul-Jabbar came and found us. In no time the whole family had arrived and they all had the chance to kiss him goodbye.

I was pleased that Mohammed died in a good way. We each gave him our forgiveness and he filled our hearts with more love and harmony than ever before. I was glad he came back. I was glad we spent his last days together and I was glad he died in my arms. His last words to me were the same words said in our wedding night, his first words ever said to me, "you are more beautiful than I had ever imagined," yet this time I didn't lower my head in shyness, instead I looked straight in to his eyes and took a last look that would stay in my heart forever.

I was sad but I was also pleased with God's will. He didn't die away, in a foreign land, with a woman who was a stranger to him as much as she was to me. He died still deeply in love with me and I with him. I was at peace; my aching heart was at peace for he was able to win my forgiveness. He was mine, always mine and he had died still mine.

His funeral took place that morning in the Manama family cemetery.

"He looked angelic and tranquil," said Abdurrahman, "he needed our forgiveness and I am glad he lived his last days among us."

"I will miss him, I will miss his humor and the happiness he brought to this house," said Looloo.

Lulwa and Noor cried in silence and Abdul-Jabbar wanted to be left alone. Doctor Ali did all the funeral arrangements and Abdulillah did the food arrangement with Yousif for all the guests who would be coming to give their condolences. The men gathered in Abdurrahman's house and the women were in my house. It was the night time that was the most difficult. Everyone would go back to their houses and I remained alone all over again, staring at the empty walls and hearing my own crying echo. It was all quiet again as it was the day Mohammed left me the first time, but this time I was not angry, I was not hurt. I was thankful to God for answering my prayers and bringing my beloved back to me even though it was for a short time; it made up for all the past.

★

Mohammed's death left me in a deep sorrow and isolation. I wished he had stayed with me forever. I wished he had never left. I missed him; I missed his smile, his healing words. I missed it all but I was glad he was resting in peace.

I spent the next four months and ten days at home, in a mourning period we called *Idda*. The Muslim widow mourns for four months and ten days, during which she leaves her house only for an emergency and has no contact with male strangers. There are many reasons for such a rule, but personally it gave me time to rebuild myself, my faith, my strength, and what remained from my life.

"Mama, this is the last day of your *Idda* what do you want to do today?" Noor asked me.

"It passed so quickly," I said in wonder.

"Do you love my grandfather so much that you didn't notice all the time that passed?" asked Sarah, Fatima's daughter.

"My whole life passed without me noticing it, dear child, someday you will realize that too and will remember me."

"Well, Mama, what do you want to do?" asked Abdurrahman.

"Take me to the beach," I commanded.

"The sea?" they all said in surprise.

"Yes. I want to wash all my sadness away and throw it in the sea."

"Why, Grandma?" asked Mariam's youngest daughter in an innocent way.

I walked towards her, carried her, kissed her and said, "So the waves carry it far away from me and my family until the day I die."

The children gave me my wish and I was comforted. It really felt like throwing my troubles away and my heart was bidding the pain farewell.

It felt good. It was a relief. And I loved watching it go away between the white foam as the winter wind brushed against my hair with promises of a better tomorrow.

I walked into my home with dignity. I knew I had won the challenge. I knew I had won my fight with time. I had all that my heart desired and I was proud of it. I saw my children's tearful eyes and dried them with a smile. There was nothing more I wanted now, nothing at all.

Chapter Eighteen

My grandchildren? Yes, it is true when they say that your grandchild is more precious than your own child. It was when Mohammed died that Sarah moved in with me. She was sixteen, crazy, adventurous and curious about everything. She had many dreams. Some she was able to accomplish, some remained a dream to be shared by the two of us.

Sarah and I were close. We would spend the whole night talking about the past, about the future, her future.

"I want to fall in love, Yummah," she would tell me. "Were you ever in love?"

My story with Mohammed was her favorite; she even took some of his old stuff to keep as a memory. We were about to complete our two years together when the inevitable happened. We both knew it was going to happen, we both denied it until we couldn't any more.

Yummah, that's what my grandchildren came to call me, like Mama, how beautiful was that?

"Yummah, they want me to leave," she said with tearful eyes and shaky voice.

"It's okay my little girl, it's only for your best."

"But I don't want to go. I want to stay right here. Why? Why do I have to do something I don't want to do?"

I did not know what to say for I didn't want her to leave either. She was graduating in two months and then off to Boston, to university thousands and thousands of miles away. I never understood why a girl would leave her family and go to the other end of the world for education when we had one here. I know it's not as good but was it really worth it? Both her parents believed so and I couldn't object. But I had faith in my little girl and I knew she was going to be okay.

And she was. She was gone. She was alright but never got used to it and never liked it. The first time she came home after that was a surprise, for she came back with her *hijab*.

"I needed to wear it, Yummah, it is a weird world and I was scared. I needed to be closer to God and I found myself attached to the idea of *hijab* every day."

I always expected her to wear it, but the fact that she did so in the United States was the surprise and I was happy for her, yes I was, for there was nothing better than having a strong faith and challenging the world with it, especially in a strange world away from your own.

I would wait for her return but there was something in my heart that told me she would never live here again. She would never come to live with me again or even sleep over sometime. She would never be close to me again though our hearts would never part. We would never stay up all night to share intimate secrets or wake each other up for *fajr* prayers. We would never laugh at our own jokes or count the stars on a clear night. It would never be the same.

And I was right. It was her second year in Boston and Sarah came back for summer. We were in Mecca, Doctor Ali took us all for the weekend and Sarah and I shared a room together.

"Yuma, it happened, it finally did." she surprised me.

"What did?"

"I am in love. I feel it there inside me, that ticklish funny feeling that brings so much laughter and happiness with it."

"Who is he? Where did you meet him?"

Yes, she was in love; my Sarah was finally in love. I still remember her face the first time she told me all about it. Her eyes were twinkling, her cheeks were red, her shy smile didn't leave her face and I could nearly hear her heart beat. She was so in love that she started dancing around the room singing the same love songs her mother used to sing when she fell in love with her father. What a small world; it was just yesterday when Fatima told me about her love and now it's her daughter.

It was September 30, 1999; we were all in Jeddah, Saudi Arabia, for her wedding, for she married a Saudi Arabian. It was a good night, the sky was clear, the stars had a special twinkle, it was a night like my wedding night, a happy night full of promises and dreams. I sat between my daughters, looking at them one by one. They were all married. I remember each and every wedding but this was a special night, I felt it there in my heart, there was something exceptional about this night.

It was at that moment, when the drums started beating loudly and the flowers were thrown from all direction. The flower girls in their Bahraini *thoubs* walked in dignity and the burning *incense* spread like magic. There she was, dressed in white, with a six meter train and a pearl and diamond tiara. Her smile was radiant, her heart was overjoyed. It was at that moment when I realized that nothing was ever going to be the same again. It was as I had expected, Sarah had left us for good, never to return. Never was she going to come back to live with me again as I had waited, never would she run to me to hear another story or share another secret. Her dream came true, she was in love and had a fairy tale wedding, but my dream was shattered. I was not going to watch her grow in front of my very own eyes; she was always going to be away, far away. Her visits were never going to be enough to celebrate and enjoy her return. It was never going to be the same.

Two years later her first born arrived, the family's favorite, baby Maya. She was happy, or I believed she was, and when it came to Sarah I was always right. There was one thing, one thing was wrong. Though she would never admit it her eyes screamed it. She missed home; she missed her home, her family, her old life. She loved her husband but she also loved her little island, the way I used to love this island. It was difficult and only I understood that. Her Aunt Dana lived away with her James, her sister was still away doing her Master's, her uncle returned to Dubai, but for Sarah it was different. She must have loved her husband so much that she gave up her home for it, but home is where the heart is and she couldn't deny it. I only wished her husband would understand the way I do what Sarah had to give up to be with him, only then would my heart rest and I would know that she is in good hands.

"Yummah, we are going to Dubai," said Sarah one Friday morning. She had made it into a habit of hers to call every Friday morning from Jeddah.

"Why is everyone going to Dubai all of a sudden?"

"We think it's better for us."

"Why don't you come to Bahrain?"

"You know how much I love Bahrain but Yummah, we need to be on our own. We need to be away from family and their interference. We need to feel independent. We are still young but we lead a life of old people."

"What can I say? I was hoping you would come back here someday, but I also understand that you need to do this."

"I love you, Yummah, and I was hoping you would come with us."

"And leave my wonderful home?"

"Only for a while. Please, Yummah."

"I am an old woman now, Sarah."

"Where is this woman's spirit, the thing I adored in her the most?"

Sarah always had her way no matter what. I did not want to go to Dubai, not only because I was old and didn't want to be a burden on anyone, but because I have lost loved ones in Dubai. I didn't want to see the place though I was filled with curiosity, but Sarah made up her mind and there was nothing that would change it.

★

It was a beautiful March afternoon. The plane landed in Dubai International Airport. I took my first steps on these lands not knowing if it would be a good or a bad experience. I felt cold, numb in a way. I felt adventurous, I felt envious, for these lands took my husband away. I have always imagined it to be a small place for some reason but the airport alone was bigger than my Bahrain. People were busy, rushing away, passing by me without even noticing I existed. They did a million things all at the same time; talked on the mobile phones, wrote stuff, carried their luggage with passports in their hands and rushing to the passport control area. I watched as I followed like a small lost turtle, wondering why they took life so seriously and put themselves under so much stress and pressure. Life could be so simple only if they allowed it to be. But then again this was the new generation, the know-all generation.

"Madam, do you need any help?" asked a gentleman.

"If you could be kind enough to tell me where I should go for my luggage?" I said shyly, feeling like a teenager.

"Can I have your passport? I will be happy to help you."

"Please don't bother yourself, son, you can just show me and I can find my way."

"This is my job, madam, to help you. It will be an honor."

Sarah was waiting impatiently outside with her daughter. The weather was hot and sticky. I was tired and the humidity made me feel suffocated under the *abaya* but I was happy to see my grand daughter. From all the people who know me she was the only one who knew what it really meant to me to be in Dubai, and she knew exactly what it was I wanted to see.

"Yummah, we are going on a trip, just you and me," she said a couple of days later.

"Where to?"

"A special trip I was planning for a while now."

Even though she wouldn't tell me, my heart knew where I was going. I was waiting for this trip; I had imagined it for so long now that I really wanted to see the real thing.

I watched the streets of Dubai. I studied every corner, every landmark, every road, imagining Mohammed walking past them or sitting next to them. I studied every café, every mosque and every house, wondering if he had ever visited them or stopped in for some business. I watched the faces of old men, wondering if they ever knew him, if they were his friends one time, if they knew he had died and that he had died in my arms not in the arms of another woman. We stopped by the creek where many tourists gathered, waiting for the *dhow*. I didn't know why she brought me here, I didn't understand the meaning of the place until I heard the tour guide explaining to his group how this was the main port many years ago, it was the only port.

"Yes, Yummah, this is where my grandfather took his first steps," she said as she held me tightly.

I looked around speechless. It was quite different than I had expected but then again so much must have changed since that time. I could see him clearly there in front of me. He was young, he was handsome, but he was sad. I know he was sad. He had nothing. He had left it all in Bahrain. I remember.

"Are you alright?" she asked.

"He must've felt lonely."

"He was lonely."

"I wish he had never left."

I walked towards the car remembering the day he had left. The memory of it all was so fresh that it felt like yesterday. It was a silent drive, as if Sarah knew I needed this moment for myself. It was what I liked best about her, she knew me too well.

I was deep in thought when the car suddenly stopped in front of a big mansion. There were big gates with guards and a big garden. The fence had flags all around it. It looked like a cathedral with its stone walls and colorful windows. This was the house Mohammed lived in when he first married Amina. It might've been a grand mansion to him, something that tempted him to marry her, but to me it was nothing more than a prison. It looked haunted, there was no sign of happiness in these walls, no sign of life or passion, no sign of a love story that once took place behind them. Everything in this house was dead, just like their marriage. Of course, today this mansion is only an embassy, which explained the guards and flags, but it was an angry place, a bad place, just how I had imagined it.

From these impressive roads we headed to a smaller neighborhood. The street was narrow and the houses were old. There was no greenery only a couple of pine trees or so. The children playing were barefoot and everyone seemed to stare. We stopped in a corner and had to walk to our next destination for it was too narrow to drive.

We stopped in front of a very old house. It was a two-story house. The smell was nauseating and the floor was dirty with mud and filth. Sarah knocked on the door and entered as I followed. We walked up the stairs to a blue cracked door and at the first knock Amina opened the door.

Not only was she surprised, she was ashamed and mortified at the same time. She asked us in and rushed to the kitchen to make some tea as I took the opportunity to walk around to see where my Mohammed lived during his last days in Dubai.

The house was small and neglected. We walked into the living room which was nearly empty, with nothing but a couple of cushions and some shelves with books. There were three doors in the living room. I walked through the first and I knew right away that it must have been Faisal's room. It had a single bed, a desk and chair, some scattered papers, and a shelf filled with medicine bottles. The curtains were closed and the air was dusty. The cupboards were wide open and empty. It was a sad room. I imagined him lying in his bed, weak and sick like the day I met him. He must've needed love. He must've needed someone there with him to hold him, to comfort him. I wished I could hug him; I wished I could hold him and tell him that he would be alright. Faisal died a long time ago but it felt like yesterday when I first met him.

The second room was the girls' room. It was decorated with many dolls but none were as beautiful as my Layla. There was the smell of perfume and the double bed was covered with magazines and books and tapes. There were pictures of babies and flowers and beautiful women, probably actresses and singers, covering the walls and a picture of the girls and their father by the bedside. Mohammed was still young then but very different in a way. He looked tired, thin, and gloomy though the girls looked glamorous.

I walked towards the third room shivering. It was the room that united my husband with another woman. It was the room where they shared their intimate moments together. It was the room I hated the most and as I opened the door I burst into tears for I felt the betrayal slapping me again. It was as if he was cheating on me all over again. It was happening again at that moment; I felt the pain all over my body. Yet as I opened the door my heart was consoled when I found two separate beds, each in one corner of the room. I looked around, searching for one thing that would break my heart, but I could not find any sign of love or compassion. Everything was stiff. And there it was. The chair by the window, just how Faisal had described it, where my Mohammed sat and talked to the moon, where he ached for me and talked to me. I sat down on that chair and thought about my man. I thought about a lost love, a love that he threw away, for his pride, for vanity. I cried for all the years I spent alone and for all the years he lived in regret. I cried because I missed him, because I forgave him, because deep inside me I knew that he didn't betray me. Maybe his body did but his soul, his heart was always faithful, always.

I looked at the window and saw the bright blue sky. This is where my Mohammed would lean and search for his best friend. This is where he cried in silence and prayed for forgiveness. If only this window could talk I would have asked about the secrets it carried for me. I would have asked about his love, his tears, his sickness, his whole life without me. If only these walls could talk I would have asked about his loneliness, his grief, his memories, his pain. As I looked around there was one thing I could see clearly; Mohammed did not belong there, ever.

Amina walked with us to the car, inviting us to visit anytime, but I could see how uncomfortable she was. She knew she would never see me again but we both acted otherwise and bid each other farewell politely and we went away. That was all I wanted to see, I wanted to see my beloved's past, the past he lived without me but also with me in a way. If I had known then how much he wanted me all this time like I did now my nights would not have been so lonely.

Chapter Nineteen

Here I am, walking by myself to the end of the road. I still live in my house in Sanad. Fatima added more extensions to the house so it's much bigger and brighter. I am happy. Yes, I am happy with my accomplishments. I have a big family now that I am a great-grandmother. Aisha has six children; Khaled, Mohammed, Nasr, Faheema, Neloo, and Faiza, and sixteen grandchildren. Fatima has four girls; Amira, Sarah, Lamees, and Salma, with only one grandchild, Sarah's daughter Maya. Mariam has four as well; Manal, Marayem, Hana, and Ahmed. Dana has Suzy and Zachariah. Abdurrahman has four; Bayoon, Alia, Norah and Mohammed Jr. Lulwa has four as well; Yasser, Sumaya, Mariam, and Mohammed. Noor has Essa and Mariam and Looloo has Aisha, Faisal, Hind and is pregnant with her fourth. Abdul-Jabbar remarried and his wife just brought him Hessa, a sweet baby girl.

This is my family; nine children, thirty grandchildren, soon to become thirty-one, and seventeen great-grandchildren. A good life, difficult but good, and I am proud of it. I am proud I survived, I am proud that I didn't accept anyone's pity. I am proud that I forced the society to respect and value me after it dishonored me for being the wife whose husband walked out on her. I am proud that I taught my children how to build themselves from scratch and watched them succeed in life, and I was proud my husband died pleased with me and so there was nothing I regretted.

Layla was the only thing I had left. She sat on my rocking chair watching the wonders of life. She still played with my great-grandchildren as she did with me. She still whispered words of advice into my ears and she still was everyone's best friend, everyone's favorite as she was mine.

But like me she was ready to leave. I missed Mama; I missed my son Nader, my Hassan, and my Mohammed. I had enough of this world and now I wanted to be with them. There was nothing left for me but the counting of seconds till Layla and I are with our loved ones again.

I stood in my patio to watch them all. It was Friday afternoon and the whole family was here. It was the last day of Ramadan, we were all fasting. The servants were busy cooking, the children were playing and the adults were sitting around the table praying, reading, and meditating.

Ramadan came once a year and we would fast for a whole month, not eating or drinking from dawn to dusk. It was a time of peace, a time of prayer and devotion. It was the favorite time for every Muslim. The mosques would fill with worshippers and the poor were fed all over the country. It was a month of sharing, of love.

I couldn't believe Ramadan was over; it was already the last day. The sun was setting low and my whole family gathered around the *sufra* to eat. We heard the cannon fire – it was the signal for breaking the fast – followed by the *maghreb* prayers. We each started with dates, for it was how the Prophet Peace Be Upon Him broke his fast, for it was always good to imitate this great being and drink a glass of *zamzam* water.

The young girls would be first to wash up so they would prepare the praying area with *sujadhs* and we would pray together, in unity, in love, and affection the *maghreb* prayer headed by the Imam one of our own family men.

By the time we were finished, the servants would have prepared the food and we would start the fiesta bidding the holy month farewell and welcoming the celebration of *Eid*.

I knew it was my last Ramadan. I knew I would never be able to live through another Ramadan. I watched them eat; I watched them laugh as I laughed with them. The girls sat down for henna and the boys sang around them.

Lulwa and I started preparing for the *Eid* celebration and Noor started the decorations. It was a beautiful time, a time I had shared with Mama and my brothers, with Mohammed and my children, many years of memories, good memories.

I stayed up all night preparing for this day for somehow it was special for me. In no time I heard the first bird sing and the first sunlight drying the morning dew. I picked some fresh jasmine from the garden and placed it on the table and as I heard the end of the *Eid* prayer went to dress up for the occasion.

We had to wear new clothes in *Eid*; it was a tradition. I put on my new *thoub* from Fatima and Sarah came in to help me with my jewelry. She loved to dress me up, she loved to watch me in my best.

The house was soon jammed with people, all of whom were my children, their children, and their children and so on.

The breakfast was ready, the same breakfast I had fixed for Mohammed the morning after our wedding. *Mashmoum* filled the room with aroma and the jasmine added its sweetness to the ambiance. Distant family members came to visit and the children enjoyed their *Eidiah*, money given to children during *Eid*.

We enjoyed *Eid*, we enjoyed the times we would gather around together and I knew I was going to miss it. We loved the *Eid* lunch which was made of rice and meat decorated with raisins and nuts and all the delicious things anyone could think of. We loved sitting out in the garden late afternoon. It was a spiritual time.

I walked back into my house to call it a night and as I looked at my family for the last time I knew that God had rewarded me and I was grateful.

Chapter Twenty

Khadeeja died in her sleep that night, the way she wanted to die, the way she wished to die, the way her mother died. She was still in her *Eid thoub* and all her jewelry. She knew she was going to die that night and she was glad she was able to live for one last *Eid*, she was glad she was able to spend her last day with her family and not die alone in a haunted house.

They watched her as she lay in her bed, like an angel. She was beautiful, she never lost her beauty through these years, through all that she went through. Her wrinkles were graceful; her hair fell on the soft pillow like waves across the ocean. She was surrounded by her life story. There were pictures of her mother with Aunt Jameela, of Nader, of her brothers, and pictures of Mohammed.

When she was taken to be prepared for the funeral arrangements her children's hearts broke into pieces. Never did they imagine life without her. She was their support, she was their protector. She was always there, always behind them, always encouraging them. She held the family together through all the difficult times and now she was gone.

The women gathered in the Manama cemetery mosque female section while the men took their places behind the Imam. Her grandchildren carried her in as they all stood up to pray for her, for the woman they all loved so dearly. She lay there in front of them all covered in white from head to toe, nothing of her was seen. As the Imam called for the start of the noon prayer their eyes filled with tears. They prayed like they had never prayed before. They cried in silence, aching for her arms, for their home.

The men and women walked side by side towards the grave. She was placed next to her husband and son. Her mother's and father's graves were close by and Hassan's grave was also there.

"At least she is not alone," said Lulwa.

"But we are," said Looloo.

She was placed facing the right side, towards the Ka'aba. The men started the burial as they bid her farewell, this time forever.

They cried. They all cried, the old and the young. Family members left but her children stayed right there besides the cold grave. They stood there in deep silence, some prayed, some thought of her, and some tried to figure out how they would go on in life without her.

They regretted leaving her alone, to live her last days in solitude. Her death was inevitable for she was old but they never saw it coming.

"Did she know how much we loved her?" asked Fatima.

"Does she know that we are aching for another day with her, just one more?" cried Noor.

It was all happening quickly and some of them were in denial. The house was soon filled with people but their eyes searched for each other, the brothers and sisters. They wanted to be together, to stay together, to support each other. They wanted to cry in each other's laps and comfort one another.

Her picture hung on the wall surrounded with her favorite, *mashmoum* and jasmine. They could still feel her there; here aroma still filled the room. Her room was as she left it. Her hair comb had a hair or two between its wooden teeth, her nightgown hung on the metal hanger. The bed sheets still took the shape of her body and the *subha* (rosemary) fell on the floor by the bedside. The windows were wide open, allowing a cool breeze into the room; the flying white curtain symbolized her pure soul as it escaped with the wind.

And like her, Layla was dead. She was sitting on the bedside but she was no more than threads and scattered pieces of cotton. She was their mother's best friend and their little sister. For all these years she had been sharing their lives and now she too was gone. They placed her with great care in a shoe box and stored her in the cupboard, with their mother's precious belongings, to stay as a memory which they would for so long hold on to.

The cupboards were unlocked; she never left her cupboards unlocked but she knew they would never be able to find the keys so she left them there. Her pills were left untouched on the dressing table; she never believed in such things, never trusted the doctors with her health. There was a sweet vibe in the room, a peaceful vibe. They knew she was happy, she was content, and she knew it was the end of her journey.

"She told me once she didn't want anything more from life, she had it all," said Abdurrahman.

And it was true. She fought all her life but saw the rewards coming in the end. She had her own palace, her own heaven where she would sit back and watch the accomplishments of her family one by one. There was nothing more she had wanted, nothing that wasn't already there. Allah was pleased with her and she was pleased with her triumph.

"This is it," said her great-granddaughter, Maya, "this is the story of our Yummah."

Made in the USA
Middletown, DE
17 February 2022